WEREN'T ANOTHER OTHER WAY TO BE

WEREN'T ANOTHER OTHER WAY TO BE

Outlaw Fiction Inspired by the Songs of

Waylon Jennings

Edited by Alec Cizak

gutterbooks.com

CONTENTS

Introduction

There comes a time in all industries, especially entertainment industries, when the drive for profit outweighs the drive for innovation and creativity. It could be said Nashville reached that point in the 1960s. Chet Atkins and several producers invented "the Nashville Sound," and artists were told what to do from then on. Today, the Nashville Sound sounds magnificent compared to the robotic, clone-like noise the industry has the audacity to call country music. The hip-hop-infused twang-infected odes to beer and corn fields hold no light to the heritage of *real* country music. Sometimes the contemporary Nashville product is called pop country, as though that will excuse it for sounding nothing like actual country music. But let's call it what it really is:

Shit.

It's shit. It's poorly digested ideas that belong in a toilet and eventually the sewer. I suspect, however, even rats would find dining on such vapid abortions of noise unfulfilling.

Apologists for this bile do what all disingenuous ball-washers do when defending such corporate abominations: They call it progress. They insult its critics by comparing the critic to an old man yelling, "Get off my lawn!" Like all empty, devoid-of-logic "arguments" made in the twenty-first century, the conflict is expected to end with the critic feeling sufficiently ashamed for not blindly going along with whatever polished turds the suits and ties foist on the public.

Waylon Jennings—or Hoss, as he was known—was disenchanted with the Nashville Sound. Imagine his opinion of the sonic vomit that Nashville floods the radio with today. One suspects the office floors of executives telling him to go with the modern flow would be littered with empty casings. The man would probably murder someone before he'd rap alongside a fiddle and steel guitar.

Hoss moved back to his native Texas to get around the Nashville Sound. He built his reputation as we currently know it recording his own tunes, his own way. The songs of Waylon Jennings are unlike any other in country music, or all popular music, for that matter. Here is a man who sang about his foibles without shame or regret. That rare performer who presented himself with no artifice. While he would eventually find the term "outlaw" useless and even problematic, there is no better word to describe him or his art.

It's quite simple: When confronted with the possibility of angering the establishment and never being allowed to work again, the artist who tells the establishment to go to hell has planted himself firmly outside of the law. At least as far as industry standards are concerned. Make no mistake, Hoss had real issues with the real law, and that's what makes him an appropriate subject for a crime fiction/noir anthology. But it's most useful to think of the word outlaw, here, as an artistic badge of honor. A middle finger to the establishment. Not many artists survive this stance. Hoss did, and that's why he's revered to this day.

I've been a part of what's sometimes called the indie crime

fiction scene for almost two decades now. In the beginning, *anything* went. As it should. Crime fiction is not a "safe space." It's a place to explore the nasty side of the human condition. Bad things happen in this arena. People are hurt. People are robbed. People are raped. People are murdered. These things happen to *all* human beings, regardless of their immutable characteristics. Your victim status on a college campus may protect you from nuanced conversations, but once you get into the real world, if someone desperate wants the contents of your wallet or purse, they're not going to stop and say, "Oh, you're a woman. Apologies. Robbing you would be misogynist. Let me move on and find someone more 'privileged' to steal from." It'd be nice if crime worked that way, but it doesn't. And the last thing we want from fiction is dishonesty.

Writers in indie crime used to know that. In recent years, however, the distasteful cult that has turned universities, Hollywood, and even the government into a preschool classroom for fragile, infantile adults has infected "the scene." Novice writers raised on the fantasies of safety and security have wedged their narcissistic snouts between publishers and the more honest writers interested in dealing with the genre in a truthful manner. This would not be a problem if they knew how to mind their own business, but they don't. This particular cult is derived from the same oppressive DNA that drove historic monstrosities such as the Salem witch trials and Manifest Destiny. They believe they know *what's best* for everyone else and they've made it their mission to eliminate any writers who deviate from their cult's deranged edicts. Questioning their dogma only leads to disingenuous platitudes about "tolerance" and "inclusiveness" by the most intolerant, non-inclusive, illiberal authoritarians to ever pollute the planet.

Gutter Books asked me to edit an anthology in which the

Pollyanna politics of the day are sharply rejected. Some might think this an invitation to publish grossly offensive stories, but that's not the purpose of outlaw fiction. Outlaw fiction, like all good fiction, takes the reader into realms they might not have the courage to explore in real life. It addresses issues polite conversation won't allow. Historically, it is out of these more uncomfortable conversations between writers and readers that *real* progress takes place. The only reason the filthy rich haven't completely locked down the world in a surveillance state is because too many people have read Orwell's *1984* and bravely continue to resist global fascism. That's the power of fiction. That's what we *should* be aiming for.

For this anthology, I chose a varied batch of stories that offer multiple points of views of the world. This diverse collection includes period pieces as well as contemporary explorations of the dirtier side of the tracks. Like many a Waylon song, they don't always conform to standard story structure. A number of Waylon tunes mysteriously fade out in the middle of a verse. Some of the stories here seem to do the same. The idea is to let the writer decide how the story should be told. Just as Waylon decided how a song should be put together.

The language may not always be pretty. The things that happen may not always be nice. Guess what? That's life. The sooner we get back to crafting fiction that reflects this, the sooner the crime fiction 'scene' will once again be dominated by creative, talented writers unafraid to tell the truth.

Alec Cizak
March 2023

WEREN'T
ANOTHER
OTHER WAY
TO BE

MICHAEL BRACKEN

WHEN SIN STOPS

Mertz, Texas, Summer 1959

Nineteen-year-old Billy Johnson and fifteen-year-old Mary Ellen Mayfield sat on the open tailgate of his father's 1953 Chevrolet Series 3100 pickup truck. His black snap-front western shirt and well-worn Wrangler jeans lay on a wool blanket in the bed behind them, his dusty boots on the ground where he'd dropped them. Sweat on his chest glistened in the mid-afternoon sun.

Unlike Billy, Mary Ellen had not fully undressed, and she smoothed her knee-length pleated skirt, adjusted her brassiere, and buttoned her white blouse. When she finished, she said, "I'm late."

Billy glanced at his watch. "We still got an hour."

"Not that kind of late," she said.

Billy had been raised by his single father—his mother had died from undiagnosed mitral valve stenosis before he became a teenager—and he didn't know of women's things. As Mary Ellen explained, his eyes grew wide. "A baby?"

She nodded.

"What're we going to do?"

"We could get married."

"You know your daddy won't allow that." Mary Ellen's father was president of the Mertz Bank and Trust, the fourth consecutive Mayfield to helm the Bank since its founding in 1846. Billy's father was the bank's security guard, a job he'd held since an automobile accident had left him with a pronounced limp.

"We could elope."

"Elope where?"

"Las Vegas," Mary Ellen said. "We can get married in Las Vegas."

Billy reached behind Mary Ellen for his jeans. "We need to get you home before the bank closes."

They didn't speak on the drive into town. Instead, Billy turned on the radio and they listened to country and western music from the AM station over in Chicken Junction. Three blocks from the Mayfield Mansion, Billy pulled his father's pickup truck to the curb. Mary Ellen leaned over, kissed his cheek, and said, "See you Thursday."

"Yeah," he said. "Thursday."

She poked him in the ribs. "You don't have to sound so excited."

He turned to face her. "I…"

"I'll do that thing you like," she said. "You just think about it until then."

This time Mary Ellen kissed him on the lips. Then she slipped out of the truck, and Billy watched until she disappeared through the antebellum home's entrance gate. He wondered if her little sister had already roused their mother from her drunken stupor or if Mary Ellen would have to prepare the martini her father expected to have waiting upon his arrival.

His own father preferred beer at the end of his workday, and he didn't like to be picked up late on the days Billy used the truck. So, Billy was sitting in the parking lot behind the bank building at five minutes before five. At precisely five o'clock, his father pushed open the rear door and held it as the bank's employees drifted out singly and in pairs. He flirted with the tellers, all of whom were young woman, and was deferential to the bank officers, all of whom were older men. The last to leave before Billy's father set the alarms and finished his shift was Mary Ellen's father, an authoritarian who wore three-piece suits at the height of summer and who never seemed to sweat.

Mr. Mayfield drove away in a white 1959 Cadillac Coupe De Ville that would be replaced as soon as the 1960 models were available. A full two minutes later, Billy's father exited the building, locked the rear door, and limped over to the truck where Billy was waiting in the passenger seat. Before climbing in, he unfastened his gun belt and tossed it onto the bench seat next to Billy. He always took his gun belt off at the end of the workday, and he often left it in the truck overnight.

A moment later, Billy's father keyed the ignition and said, "I think Sally Henderson has her eye on me."

"No way. She's closer to my age than yours."

"I was older than your mother."

"By four years, not forty."

"I may be old but I'm not dead." His father shrugged. "You hungry? I was thinking barbecue."

They stopped at Polumbry's Pit Bar-B-Q for sliced brisket and yellow potato salad, and they ate while sitting at the yellow Formica-and-chrome kitchen table in their two-bedroom brick ranch house. Billy nursed a Dr. Pepper, and his father downed the first of several beers he would consume that evening. They were halfway through the meal and had just finished a discussion about needing to replace the truck's balding tires when Billy asked, "Why'd you marry Mom?"

"I had to."

"You mean…?"

"Oh, hell no, not like that, not at our age." Billy had been a late-in-life child, born when his father was forty-four and his mother was knocking on forty's door. "Your mother was the only woman who would have me. That's why I had to marry her."

"How'd you know she was the one?"

"When I was with her, I didn't want her to leave, and when I wasn't with her, I wanted to be. And I still miss her even now."

Billy worked four days a week—Tuesday-Wednesday and Friday-Saturday—at the Conoco station, pumping gas, checking oil, and washing windows. Old Man Hearn handled most of the automotive repair, only occasionally letting Billy fix flats and change windshield wipers. He kept promising Billy he would give the young man additional responsibilities, but he'd been making the same promises since Billy dropped out of school two years earlier to work for him.

The Conoco service uniform—blue coveralls with a red and white stripe that ran from the right shoulder down to the right breast pocket, his name and the red-and-white Conoco logo embroidered over his left breast pocket—identified him as a working man, just as the uniform his father wore at the bank similarly identified him. A hat with a short black bill completed the service station's uniform, but Old Man Hearn never made him wear it.

He had never had luck with girls his own age—they weren't interested in gas jockeys who'd dropped out of high school and instead desired young men who wore suits and ties on days other than Sunday. He had realized this early on and had resigned himself to his fate until Mary Ellen entered his life. He had known of her—his father worked for her father, after all—but he had not even spoken with her until the bank's Christmas party the year she turned fifteen. She had caught him standing under the mistletoe when no one was watching and, after she kissed him, she pressed a finger to his lips and said, "You can't tell."

The following Wednesday, late the afternoon of Christmas Eve day, the Mayfield's white Cadillac had pulled into the Conoco station, mother and father in the front seat, both daughters in the back, all dressed in their Sunday best even though it wasn't Sunday. Billy filled the gasoline tank with premium, checked the oil, and washed the windows. As he stood at the driver's window, counting out Mr. Mayfield's change, Mary Ellen told her father she needed to use the restroom.

"It can wait," her father had said. "We'll be there in less than ten minutes."

"No, Daddy, it can't," Mary Ellen had insisted as she opened her door. "I need to go *now*."

Mr. Mayfield spun in his seat and glared at her. "Make it quick."

She did, and Billy was washing the windshield of Agnes Polumbry's Ford when she returned.

"Hey, you," Mary Ellen called to him, loud enough that her father could hear and in the tone of voice he was accustomed to hearing from people like the Mayfields and the Polumbrys. "You need to clean the ladies before anyone else goes in there. It's a powerful mess."

Billy watched the Mayfields drive away, finished attending to Mrs. Polumbry, and then took a mop and bucket to the ladies' restroom, expecting the worst. What he found instead was a message Mary Ellen had written on a paper towel that suggested a time and place they could meet.

Billy remembered all that, but he spent most of the time between customers thinking about all the things they had done ever since the first time she had let him reach up under her blouse. He thought about her extra hard after their conversation Monday afternoon. When he picked her up Thursday at their special place near her home, he was still thinking about what she'd said, and he was thinking about it all the way to Grover's Gully, where he parked his father's truck so it wasn't visible from the nearby highway.

Mary Ellen slid across the bench seat and dropped one hand into his lap. "You want me to do that thing?"

He stopped her by turning, placing his hands on her shoulders, and holding her at arm's length. "I thought a lot about what you said the other day. I'll marry you—I will—but what about your daddy?"

"He says I'm the woman of the house," Mary Ellen said. She pushed his hands off her shoulders and slid closer. "I'd rather be the woman of your house."

"But how will we get to Vegas?"

She didn't answer. Instead, she pushed her long black hair aside and did the thing she'd promised, driving all other questions from his mind.

Though Billy and Mary Ellen had been seeing each other since Christmas, it had been difficult during the school year to find time to be together without her father discovering their relationship. Things had been easier since the beginning of summer. Her father was at the bank all day, her mother was passed out by noon, and her little sister knew better than to say anything when Mary Ellen slipped out of the house two afternoons each week.

But her mother wasn't completely inattentive.

The following Monday, after spending time with Billy in the

bed of his father's pickup truck, Mary Ellen said, "My mother knows."

"Knows what?"

"That Aunt Flo hasn't visited," Mary Ellen said. "She counts the pads, and I haven't used one in almost eight weeks."

Billy stared at her.

"She said she knew this would happen and that there's nothing she could have done to stop it."

"She don't know about us. You told me she don't know about us. Ain't nobody knows about us."

"It doesn't matter what my mother thinks she knows," Mary Ellen said. "It isn't her problem."

"I will marry you, Mary Ellen. I promise. I just got to figure a couple things out first."

"Well, you better hurry because pretty soon I'll start showing and then everybody will know."

Old Man Hearn had gone to Polumbry's Pit Bar-B-Q for lunch on Wednesday, so Billy was alone in the Conoco station when Mr. Mayfield's white Cadillac slid to a halt out front. He headed toward the door, but Mr. Mayfield was out of the car and storming toward him.

They met in the open doorway. Billy stepped back and then stepped back again until the counter stopped his retreat.

Mr. Mayfield jabbed a finger into Billy's chest. "What have you done to my daughter?"

"I haven't…"

"Don't you lie to me, boy. You're the only one who could have."

Billy swallowed hard and straightened up. "I love Mary Ellen, and I plan to marry her."

Mr. Mayfield backhanded him. "Don't you ever let me hear my daughter's name come out of your mouth."

Billy put his hand to his cheek. "But…"

"You listen and you listen good, boy. I'll take care of your little surprise package, and you forget you ever met my daughter. You don't see her, you don't talk to her, you don't even *think* about her."

"But…"

"The only butt here is yours, and it's in a sling. You're damn lucky I'm feeling generous today or I'd take you behind the barn and shoot you for what you've done. And if you tell anyone, *anyone* at all, about this, I *will* shoot you." Mary Ellen's father grabbed Billy's crotch and squeezed so tight the young man's eyes watered. "And I'll nail these to the wall in my trophy room."

When Mr. Mayfield released his grip, Billy slid to the floor, curled into a fetal ball, and watched through tear-filled eyes as the banker drove away.

Billy was sitting in the kitchen when his father returned home. He wore nothing but his BVDs and had a dish towel filled with ice pressed against his crotch. When his father asked what had happened, Billy said, "I had an accident at work."

"You need to be a damn sight more careful." Then his father opened a beer, made himself a baloney and mustard sandwich, and went to the living room to eat it while watching the evening news.

Billy slept fitfully that night, but he woke early enough to take his father to work. Usually, he waited until his father was inside the bank before he drove away, but not that day. He left before Mr. Mayfield arrived, and he spent the morning pacing the house until it was time to meet Mary Ellen.

He waited at their special place for almost an hour and was about to give up when she finally arrived. As soon as she was in the truck and the door was closed, he sped away, hightailing it west to Grover's Gully where no one could see what they might do.

"Why were you late?" he asked.

"My mother was watching me. She usually passes out right after lunch, but not today."

As soon as he cut the engine, Mary Ellen snuggled up against him and slid her hand up the inside of his thigh.

He pushed it away. "I can't."

She slid her hand upward a second time. "Why not?"

He told her what her father had done to him the previous day. "It still hurts."

"He doesn't want you to see me anymore, and yet you came anyhow."

"Yeah."

They sat in silence for a while before she turned on the radio and tuned it to the country and western station. Then they sat for a while longer, his arm wrapped around her.

Billy returned home from the Conoco station the next day and found his father sitting in the living room, uniform shirt half unbuttoned, a beer bottle in one hand and three empties on the floor. As Billy peeled off his coveralls, wet from the light rain that had started mid-afternoon, he asked, "Why are you home so early?"

"That sonofabitch at the bank fired me."

"Mr. Mayfield? Why'd he do that?"

"He said you'd know why. Why would you know why? You done something?"

"No, I…"

His father pushed himself out of his chair and stood toe-to-toe with Billy, his beery breath washing over Billy's face when he spoke. "Don't lie to me, son."

Billy swallowed hard. "I been seeing Mary Ellen."

"His daughter?"

Billy nodded.

"She's fifteen!"

"So? Mom was four years younger than you."

"Jesus Christ, son, you ain't got the sense God gave a goose."

"It's like you told me," Billy insisted. "When I'm with Mary Ellen, I don't want her to leave, and when I ain't with her, I want to be."

"Do you know who holds the mortgage to this house? Do you know who—ah, hell, it don't matter. You just need to stop. Stop seeing her, stop talking to her, stop…"

"I can't. Not now. She's going to have a baby."

"Oh, sweet Jesus," Billy's father said. "We're fucked."

"We?"

"I didn't raise you up to be stupid, did I? What the Polumbrys don't control, the Mayfields do, and they make life hard for anybody who crosses them."

"I…" Billy had no more words.

His father limped into the kitchen and returned with two mismatched glasses and an unopened bottle of whiskey he'd received from the bank the same Christmas Mary Ellen had kissed Billy. He cracked the seal. "Look in the mirror. What do you see?"

Billy looked around even though he knew there was no mirror in the living room.

"That girl could have any boy in town, so why you? I love you, son, but you're uglier than a hound dog's ass."

"But she…"

"That girl ain't blind. She's using you."

"For what?"

"To piss off her daddy. There ain't no other reason."

"That can't be right. Mary Ellen wouldn't…"

"You're stupider than a box of rocks. She's a Mayfield. Mayfields have been using people like us since before Texas was a state." He poured three fingers of whiskey into each glass and handed one to Billy. "This'll put hair on your chest, son, and you're going to need it when you go to Mr. Mayfield and beg for forgiveness."

Billy only drank the one glass of whiskey. His father drank until he passed out, so he didn't hear the phone when it rang late that evening. When Billy answered, he heard Mary Ellen on the other end. "You have to come get me."

They had never spoken on the phone, afraid that someone would overhear. "When?"

"Tonight. It must be tonight. My father's sending me away in the morning. He won't tell me where, but you'll never see me again if you let him do that."

Billy glanced at his watch. "Midnight. I'll get you at midnight."

"There isn't time for me to get to our…"

"I'll come to the house. You be ready."

Twenty minutes later, Billy eased out of his home carrying a grocery bag filled with clothing. He also had a jar of peanut butter and the twenty-seven dollars he'd saved from his job at the Conoco. He hurried through the rain, climbed into the pickup truck, and put his sack of clothing on the other side of his father's gun belt before keying the ignition. A few minutes later he drove up the circular drive of the Mayfield Mansion and stopped in front of the porch. Except for light seeping from an upstairs window, the house was dark.

Mary Ellen had waited on the front porch, and she was dragging a heavy suitcase down the steps by the time he stopped the truck. Before Billy could climb out to help, the porch lights snapped on and Mary Ellen's father, dressed in blue silk pajamas and house slippers, rushed out of the house. He grabbed his daughter's arm just as she reached the bottom step. "She's not going with you, Billy. Not now. Not ever."

Billy pulled the revolver from his father's gun belt, climbed from the truck, and pointed it at Mr. Mayfield. The rain trickled into his eyes as he cocked the hammer. "Let her go."

"You haven't got the balls to shoot me."

Mary Ellen's father jerked her arm so hard she screamed, "Billy!"

Startled, he squeezed the revolver's trigger and Mr. Mayfield dropped to the ground.

Billy sputtered. "Oh, God, oh, Jesus, oh…"

As Mr. Mayfield tried to push himself to his feet, Mary Ellen took the revolver from Billy and told her father, "You'll never do Sissy like you done me."

Then she shot him in the head.

The truck slid on the driveway as they sped away. In the rearview mirror, Billy saw Mary Ellen's mother kneel beside her husband. Her little sister stood in the open doorway.

"We done it," Mary Ellen said as she slid across the bench seat and pressed against him. She dropped a hand into his lap. The other still held his father's revolver. "We're going to Las Vegas."

Billy headed west out of town, exceeding every posted speed limit. "I didn't mean to do it. I just wanted him to let you go. But you…you…"

"He deserved it, Billy, for what he did to me."

"What he did to you?"

"You think you were the first?"

Before he could respond, she turned on the radio and tuned in the country and western station over in Chicken Junction. Waylon Jennings's latest release on the Brunswick label filled the truck's cab.

And then flashing red lights lit up the truck and the irritating scream of a police siren pierced through the music. Billy glanced in the rearview mirror and saw a Mertz police car gaining on them. He eased his foot off the accelerator and looked for a place to pull over.

"What are you doing?" Mary Ellen demanded. She spun around to see the police car on their tail. Then she put her foot on top of Billy's and pressed until the accelerator was flat against the floor.

Billy had traveled the road toward Grover's Gully often enough that he likely could have driven it blindfolded, but the rain had slickened the road and the truck's near-bald tires slid with every turn.

A second police car joined the first.

Mary Ellen spun around again. "You can't let them catch us." She pressed the barrel of his father's revolver into his ribs. "They'll separate us. They won't let you see me ever again."

Billy glanced in the rearview mirror, seeing for the first time in her eyes what his father saw. "Just like your daddy wouldn't?"

"Just like."

"Do you love me?"

"Of course, I love you," she said.

"Do you trust me?"

She lowered the revolver. "With all my heart."

He didn't believe her. He believed his father. She was a Mayfield. She had used him, and she would keep using him until he was all used up. But he loved her despite all that. "Then we'll be together forever."

Ahead, the highway swept left and a dirt road to the right, now muddy from the rain, led down toward Grover's Gully. He knew he couldn't make the turn, so as the highway swept left, he slammed on the brakes and spun the steering wheel hard to the left. The bald tires slid on the wet pavement. The right side of the truck slid off the pavement. The tires caught in the muddy shoulder. The truck flipped over and barrel rolled into the Gully, crushing the cab and everything in it.

Tom Hoisington

Lonesome, On'ry and Mean

We were driving Cole out behind the *old* processing plant, the one by where Summit Boulevard and Manson Boulevard intersect. Tied up and gagged in the bed of the truck, we couldn't hear him where we sat up in the cab.

"You know he's back there leaking DNA evidence all over?" I asked Chevy.

"Nobody is going to DNA swab the truck," he told me. "You watch too much TV, *cabron*."

Chevy was Native, not Mexican, so every time he cursed in Spanish it sounded fake, like a put on. Another instance of him trying to pass or belong in what was supposed to be his own country.

The truth was there wasn't likely to be a DNA swab of the back of the truck because nobody would need that much help figuring out who'd killed Cole in the first place. All of the breadcrumbs would lead right to Chevy. If they wanted to look for an accomplice, I was sure they would settle on me. Chevy didn't have any other friends.

"Is that sack of potatoes still down there?" he asked me, gesturing to the floor by my feet. Chevy drove and I rode shotgun. I sifted through the wrappers and empties that always sat on the floor in Chevy's cab until I found a paper shopping bag that was heavy. Looking inside, I found three baking potatoes.

"Yeah, we got potatoes," I told him. "Why, you hungry?"

"No, gonna need one."

"For what?"

"For a suppressor, *puta madre*," Chevy said. "A silencer. There's that winery out here that's not too far from the plant."

"That thing's been closed for a while."

"Yeah, well I'm not taking any chances," Chevy said.

It reminded me of the time in high school when we had roomed together for the Mat Classic. In Washington State, the wrestling state championship is held every year at the Tacoma Dome. Somehow, four of us from our tiny high school had qualified and, of course, the two white kids roomed together while me and Chevy were left to room together.

Not that we minded. We were teammates and acquaintances at that point, not as close as we would eventually become, but we sure as shit didn't want to room with the white kids. What would we have to talk about? It would be awkward as fuck. Coach Lenny and Coach Logan took the third room.

It was on that trip that Chevy and I became really close. *Carnal.* I had been in bed watching boxing on ESPN2 knowing there was no way I was going to be able to fall asleep while stressing about the tournament the next day when Chevy pulled out *la mota* and an apple he had stashed from lunch.

"C'mon," he had said, pulling out his pocketknife. "We have to go down to the parking garage."

"What the fuck are you doing with an apple?" I had asked him.

"I'm going to smoke this," he said, holding up the *mota*, "out of this," he said, holding up the apple.

"How?" I had asked him.

"If you get off your ass and come with me, I'll fucking show you," he said.

And now, four years later, we were going to use a potato as a suppressor. Chevy knew his produce.

"Yo, you with me, *puta*?" Chevy asked me. He had noted me spacing off as we wound our way up the lake. Chevy had only ever bothered to learn the Spanish curse words. His hair was jet black and his ochre skin sometimes led Anglos to believe that he was Mexican, or sometimes Latinos would come up and start jabbering to him in Spanish. He would stare at them blankly. The dirty words were all he knew.

"*Si, claro,*" I said. We had snatched Cole in the bowling alley parking lot in Chelan and now were taking him up WA 150 to the village of Manson, where the three of us had attended high school and been raised and, if Chevy could go through with it, where Cole was going to end tonight.

"You need a drink or something?" he asked me. "Get your heart up a little bit?"

"My heart is fine," I told him. "Watch the road. And follow the speed limit."

WA 150 wound along the coastline of Lake Chelan. Every year during tourist season, without fail, some drunk from west of the mountains on vacation would miss a turn and find their Hummer submerged in the lake. If they were just *pretty* drunk the cold glacial water woke them up, and they swam their ass to shore to call a tow truck. If they were *really* drunk then they drowned and the tow truck took longer to come, not until someone realized the people were missing or somebody spotted the trunk of the SUV jutting up out of the shallow water near the shoreline.

"He's had this coming for a long time, Iggy," Chevy said. "Tonight is just the night."

I didn't answer him. Cole was a racist asshole piece of shit, but he didn't deserve to die, any more than any of the other racist assholes in the county did. Were we going to get all of them now? We wouldn't get far. Most of them had a lot of guns, and white people in Chelan county didn't need potato silencers to shoot Mexicans and Natives.

A few years back at My Buddy's Place some biker had followed a Native out the door, tailed his truck on his bike, forced him off the road, and then beat the Native to death. It was still officially "unsolved," but all of the bikers and all of the Natives saw them have beef with one another and then leave within five minutes of each other. Everybody in those two communities knew exactly what had happened, and they were the two groups of people least likely to tell any of it to the Chelan Sheriff's Department.

"We've all got a lot coming," I told him. "Are we the ones dishing it out now?"

"We are tonight," he told me.

"Well, I hope it's worth it," I told him. "After the fact."

"It will be worth it that Cia doesn't have to see his piece-of-shit ass around town anymore," Chevy said.

And there you had it. The oldest reason to shoot motherfuckers in the history of shooting motherfuckers. Somebody fucked your girl. And before they invented shooting, they used to stab each other for it. Tale as old as time.

Chevy and Lucia had been on-and-off together since grade school, is what you had to understand. Lucia's dad and mom came up one season to pick apples in the orchards and her dad was such a good worker that they hired him on as a foreman so he could stay year-round. The owner of the orchard gave the family their own little house away from the pickers' bunks and through the winter and spring Lucia's dad would first prune and then mind the trees, getting them ready for summer and then managing the picking crews in the fall.

Lucia was the third of four kids. Her parents really couldn't even afford one kid, but you can't talk to old school Catholics like that. "Go forth and multiply," or something. As if finding a method of birth control so that you didn't have to starve with double-digit kids was some kind of betrayal of the grand design.

Cole had been with us in school from the beginning also. His folks were orchardists; they owned the Lucky 13 Orchards that overlooked the lake. The summer between elementary school and middle school, Cole's parents sold the orchard to some developers who were going to rip up the trees and chop it up into lots to build vacation homes for Microsoft and Amazon executives who wanted to escape the relentless drizzle west of the mountains.

After Cole's dad got ahold of that money, he about quit doing anything. He was "set for life," as he used to tell everybody at My Buddy's Place. Pretty soon he was screwing around on Cole's mom and then pretty soon after that they got a divorce. Then Cole's dad married again to somebody only about seven years older than us and gave him a little brother that Cole's dad seemed to like a lot better than Cole himself to go with the stepmom who couldn't stand the sight of Cole.

Cole's mom got away with half the developer's money and began hitting the sauce pretty hard, too, after the divorce. You could tell it affected Cole because whereas before he was just a little bit arrogant—our little blondie in a sea of brown skin and black hair—after that he just got downright mean. Cruel. Pulling really hurtful pranks and saying really mean shit, just for fun.

Until one day he tried it with the wrong guy. That would be Chevy.

Look, we all three of us wrestled. I don't know why. Truth be told, Cole was one of those two white kids I mentioned who made it to Mat Classic with us. I just don't like to admit it and give him credit for accomplishing anything, putting his nose down and working for anything.

And we all know they don't give you anything in wrestling. It doesn't matter who your dad is or what he sold and how much money he got for it. That might get you some snaps in football, some minutes in basketball, or some ABs in baseball. In wrestling, putting somebody out there when they don't belong isn't doing them any favors. They would just get their face ground into the mat and embarrassed in front of, if we're honest, a mostly empty gymnasium. That's just the nature of the sport.

Wrestling in our school district began in seventh grade and the three of us took to it immediately. By eighth we were all cemented as junior high varsity starters having overtaken the guys a year older in each of our weight classes. While that might sound impressive, wrestling in Washington State is a small pond. You don't have to be particularly talented, just dedicated. Committed.

In the first meet back after Christmas, Cole took some dog shit and put it in Chevy's wrestling shoe, then him and the white ninth graders watched as Chevy slid his socked foot into it. They busted up laughing as the look of confusion and then disgust spread across Chevy's face.

This, again, was nothing personal against Chevy. Cole acted like this to everybody. He had some deep-seated resentment against his dad and the world in general that he was working out in unhealthy ways. But Chevy came from a dad and a world of resentments, too.

Cole couldn't have known that Chevy worked all through the summer in ninety-five degree heat for a landscaping company to afford those shoes. That he had had his heart set on the black and yellow Rulons and had indeed gone out and got them.

It was neither of their faults. It was unstoppable force/immovable object. Just two cars coming together at an intersection. But come together they did.

Chevy whipped his shoe and sock off while the white boys were still laughing and, to me, not even being that tight with Chevy at that point, I had to wonder why Cole wasn't bracing up. Anybody who knew anything about Chevy knew what was about to happen next. Maybe Cole thought being Anglo or having money absolved him of that?

But it didn't. Chevy hit him like a ram with his famous blast double, the best one on the team. Cole went tumbling ass over tea kettles into the lockers behind him, the back of his skull making a sickening "crack" when it connected with the bottom door.

Before the other white guys could pull him off, Chevy was smearing the shitty sock all over Cole's face.

"How's that taste, you little fucking bitch?" he asked him, not yelling, scarily calm, hissing through his teeth. "Did you get that shit from your mom's pen? Your pale pink ass looks just like your pig mom you little fucking cunt."

Blood was streaming from the back of Cole's head and his face was covered in dog shit by the time the coaches came rushing in.

Cole got a two-week suspension. Chevy got thrown off the team for the rest of the eighth-grade year. In ninth they let him come back on a probationary period but, even though they were pretty close in size, the coaches made sure Chevy and Cole never drilled together.

For a while in ninth Cole would glare across the mat at Chevy, but Chevy just studiously ignored him. For Cole, wrestling was just another sport. He also played football in the fall and ran the eight hundred in the spring.

For Chevy, wrestling was all he did. It was his identity at the school. In the off seasons when he wasn't working he would hit a dusty old heavy bag out behind his dad's house or go for long runs in the roads that wound up and through the orchards.

Cole played wrestling. Chevy didn't *play* wrestling. For kids closer to the survival line, playing wasn't so much an option, which is why abstractions like balls and sticks didn't make sense to us. You strip us down and stand us across from another guy, though, and tell us one of us has to take the other one down and then hold him down? That makes sense. Chelan County had been trying to take and hold us down our whole lives.

WA150 turned into Main Street Manson and Chevy dropped his speed for the drive through town. The laundromats and cafes were dark. My Buddy's Place was the only place loud with the lights on, smokers spilling out the front door and Hank Williams Jr. singing loudly from the jukebox within.

As we drove by, Chevy was careful to avoid eye contact with anybody there who might recognize him. He didn't want anyone to be able to say they saw him passing through town at this hour.

"*Pinche gringos*," Chevy muttered under his breath. I looked away from the bar too. It was doubtful that anyone could see into the darkened cab, but they wouldn't need to. This was Chevy's truck. Probably the only 1978 Toyota long bed still functioning on the West Coast.

We hadn't stolen a new car that wouldn't be recognized for this gig. We weren't that smart.

"We're gonna shoot all them too?" I asked him, still looking away from him, looking out the window.

He scoffed. "Wouldn't be a bad idea."

I just shook my head. He was mad at the whole world, mad at his whole life, and Cole had always been the one stupid enough to get in his crosshairs. Some of these motherfuckers just have to prove they have it over you and won't stop until you get it through your thick skull.

But Chevy never got it through his skull. He preferred to rearrange other people's skulls. Sometimes with lockers, sometimes with potato-suppressed pistols.

I think college would have been good for any of us. For all of us. Me and Cole and Chevy, none of us were good enough to wrestle at any of the West Coast Division One colleges that still had wrestling programs, but we could have given it a go at a community college or junior college.

The problem was that would have involved going west of the mountains at the very least or maybe as far as Oregon or, gasp, California, and I think that was just beyond our imaginations, for admittedly different reasons.

Chevy's ancestors were from the region, so maybe he had the most legitimate reasons for staying. And after he graduated high school and lost the structure that wrestling gave him, he *did* get into the closest thing to tribal politics. He started working at the Mill Bay Casino.

They tried him at a few different gigs—dealer, server. But he didn't smile and his customer service was shit and he had never been all that good at math so, eventually, as small as he was, they took one look at his ears, crumbled and misformed by years of wrestling practice without headgear, and put him where he had always belonged: Security. Chevy was unafraid to take on anyone of any size. In fact, most nights, he was spoiling for a fight. And so the tribe gave him an outlet to channel that aggression into.

He and Cia moved in together, him paying his half of the rent from his security gig and her with tips from various waitressing shifts she picked up at the resorts and restaurants and bars around town. And, for a while, they were happy like that. Nobody would mistake it for the *Lifestyles of the Rich & Famous*, but they weren't starving and they had a roof over their head. Cia's family lived close and they had weekends and holidays with them. Were maybe ready to start thinking about kids of their own when they got more settled in a couple years.

I picked up seasonal gigs during those years. Worked the harvests. Got on at the packing plant and drove a forklift in the deep freeze of the storage facilities, piling on the insulated Carhartt gear even as the pleasant weather of late September and early October descended on the high plains of Eastern Washington. I found my way onto crews of landscaping companies in the spring and summer, hung Christmas lights in the late fall and winter. Even with that meager work I could afford a place of my own back then. The property values hadn't totally skyrocketed yet. Working folks could still somehow scrape by.

And Cole mostly took after his dad. He sucked money off his parents, both of them, that sweet developer money trickling down to his recreational activities. He tried to start businesses. A fishing guide company. A snowmobile rental company. None of them ever made any money, but it gave him an excuse to mooch more cash off his parents without actually putting his head down and working at anything.

It seemed Cole was content to be the drunken prince of upper Lake Chelan. There was nothing but opportunity out there waiting for a white kid with a nice smile and some financial backing, but he never seemed to want to take advantage of any of it. He wanted to hang around My Buddy's Place and plow lake tourists in the summer and snowmobile bunnies in the winter. He wanted to have a place of his own but also access to his mom and his dad's spreads whenever he might need more space. You might say he was hesitant to leave the nest. *Failure to launch* is another term.

So with all of that the case, you might rightfully ask why Cia started up an affair with Cole one summer. Why she left Chevy and moved in with Cole, breaking Chevy's heart, damn near killing him.

We all knew why Cole had done it. Cole did it to get back at Chevy for the shitty sock smeared all over his face and any number of scowls and mini confrontations that had gone between them over the years. Cole's frail ego needed everyone to kowtow to him, and Chevy refused to give him any kind of deference whatsoever.

So when Cole saw the opportunity to steal Chevy's girl, have her around the house to fuck for a few months before cutting her loose and then, hopefully, having Chevy take her back so they would all know, all three of them know, always know, that Cole had taken what was rightfully Chevy's whenever he had wanted to, well, that was all too in character for Cole.

But I never understood why Cia did it. I asked her about it a few years later, after all of this was over, the truck ride up lake and all of that. I asked her what good she thought was going to come out of shacking up with Cole for a few months. And couldn't she see that she was just a pawn in a long running feud between the two of them?

"I guess I knew that on some level," she said to me when I had enough cervezas and tequilas in me to ask. "But I didn't admit it to myself. I wanted to believe that he liked me for me."

"That Cole did?"

"Yeah," she said. "That's right.

"Even though he regularly ran around here every year fucking tourists from the westside with fake tits and Pilates asses?"

Cia was a sweet enough kid, but she was no supermodel. She was on the Indian side of Mexican herself, which is why, physically, she and Chevy had always seemed a good match.

"Yeah, I know," she said. "If you want something bad enough you lie to yourself about why it's happening."

"What did you think you and Cole were going to do?" I asked her. "When you were lying to yourself?"

She shrugged. "You know. Get out of here. Go somewhere else. Do something else. See something different. This is all I've ever known, the only place I've ever been. Me and my family never went on vacation or anything."

It was true. Cia and her family had stayed confined to the valley as long as I'd known them. Her father's parents and even some siblings had died back in Mexico and, close a family as they were, he had never even scraped the money together to go back to the old country for their funerals, let alone had cash lying around for leisure travel.

You couldn't blame her. She saw Cole and his interest in her as her one shot at something else. Somewhere else. So she took the chance, even though she knew, and we all knew, what the outcome was likely to be.

And when Cole did, inevitably, tell her to pack her shit and get out, Chevy of course took her back. Because he couldn't bring himself to blame her, either. And after that, every time they saw each other around town, Cole didn't scowl at Chevy anymore. He *sneered* at him. Knowingly. And that might seem not to be that much of a difference, a scowl versus a sneer, even a knowing sneer, unless you've lived in the same town all your life with the same set of motherfuckers and you know all of the words that go into and behind that knowing sneer.

Chevy took months of those sneers. More than I thought he was capable of, to be honest. For a week or two, I thought that this might be the thing that got him and Cia out of town. That he would get so sick of the sneers that he would finally have the motivation and desperation to take her and get the fuck out of this county.

But he came up with another solution. Because the last time, the time we were on our way out of the bowling alley and Cole was on his way in, and he made dead-lock eye contact with Chevy and gave him his best knowing sneer yet, Chevy and me got in his truck, but Chevy didn't put the key in the ignition.

We sat there for a beat.

"Are we going?" I eventually asked him.

"No," he said.

"Then what are we doing?" I asked him.

"We're waiting," he told me. "Waiting for that *gringo* asshole."

And that's what we did. And when Cole came out the front door of the bowling alley, waved goodbye to his friends, and turned up the alley, alone, toward his house, just like Chevy knew he would, Chevy was right behind him with his pistol and a roll of duct tape.

And that was how Cole woke up in the back of Chevy's truck with a massive cranial contusion and his wrists and ankles bound with duct tape on a one-way trip up to the old processing plant.

Cole was awake by the time we pulled into the deserted old plant and drove back behind the loading docks where no one could see us. You could hear him rolling around and kicking in the bed of the truck, but we knew we had taped him up good and that he wouldn't get loose.

We pulled into park and Chevy killed the engine and cut the lights. Then he took a half pint of Jack Daniel's out of the back pocket of his jeans, took a long gulp, and handed it to me. I put it to my lips, then took a brief moment to shake my head before taking a long drink from it.

Chevy noticed the gesture. "You should go," he told me as I was drinking. "I don't want you to get caught up in this."

Whiskey almost shot up my nose from laughing. And I had to cough and sputter to keep from choking.

"Oh, *now* you want to spare me all of this?" I asked him. "After everybody has seen us together all night and driving in your truck together through Chelan and then Manson? *Now* is the time you think I shouldn't have to be involved?"

He shook his head sadly as I passed him the bottle back. He polished it off in three long swigs.

"I wasn't thinking," he said, after he was done drinking. "I'm sorry."

I scoffed again and shook my head while looking out the passenger side window. It was dark, but I knew the orchards were out there. Rows of trees cascading over rolling hills. In the daytime they're inevitably contrasted against blue skies. Chelan is in the rain shadow of the Cascade Mountain range. There are three hundred sunny days a year.

"It's not like in the movies," he said. "I didn't have it all planned out like Danny Ocean. I just got fed up with his shit and smacked him over the head."

"Fuck it, cut him loose," I told him. "You're not like duty-bound to shoot him here."

Chevy just shook his head. "That's just another thing for him to sneer at me about," he said. "That I didn't have the balls to do him when I had him."

"I don't think you're going to have to worry about it for a while," I told him. "You'll still be doing a few years behind the assault and kidnapping."

Chevy shook his head again. "No, he won't press charges. He'll say it was just boys being boys so he can keep seeing me around town and giving me his look."

At that Chevy tried to imitate Cole's sneer. And he did a pretty good job, actually. As if he'd been seeing it often lately. As if it'd been taking up a lot of his head space.

"You can't shoot him, Chevy," I told him. "You know you can't."

"Like fuck I can't," he said, and opened the door with one hand while he picked up the gun with the other. Like a shot he stalked to the back of the truck, opened and threw down the tailgate, then grabbed Cole by the tape binding his ankles together and pulled him off the truck bed and into the dirt, where he landed with a thud and a groan.

"*Fuck*," Cole said. The truck bed was not high but bound up like that he was unable to brace himself for the fall. It must have knocked the wind out of him on top of the oozing mound of bruise on the back of his head.

Chevy grabbed the ankle tape again and began dragging Cole back behind the loading dock where anybody passing by on the road would be unable to see. We weren't likely to have any company this time of night on this stretch of road, but why take the chance, I guess he figured.

When he got to the side of the loading dock's ramp he spun Cole around and propped Cole up so he was sitting against the mound of dirt that supported the ramp. I had to admit, if he was just planning on scaring Cole—and me—then he was doing a pretty convincing job of setting up to shoot him. The mound of dirt would catch the bullet after it passed through Cole's head. It would be easy to retrieve and dispose of it. No evidence left around for ballistics.

After he set up Cole how he wanted him, Chevy leaned up against the hood of the car to breathe and sweat for a while. He wasn't in wrestling shape anymore. None of us were. It had been a long time since we had moved and manipulated bodies for fun and fitness.

"You know," Cole said, slurring slightly, probably concussed, "you're a pussy. You're not going to do shit."

"God*damn*it," I said, seeing my last chances of talking Chevy out of this slipping away.

"He *is*, Pato," Cole said to me, calling me by my wrestling nickname. My feet used to splay out when I wrestled. The coaches tried to correct my form but it was just my natural stance.

"He's not going to do shit because he's a little bitch and always has been," Cole continued. "That's why people can fuck his girl and turn her out to their friends and he won't do fuck all about it."

"Cole, *shut up* man," I told him.

"She didn't do that," Chevy said. "She wouldn't do that."

"She doesn't know *what* the fuck she did, man, and if she tells you different she's a fucking liar," Cole said. "She'd never done coke before, never done ecstasy before. If she's passed out in my house she doesn't know who did what, does she? Just me and fifteen of my closest buddies."

Chevy stared up at the stars. I couldn't tell if he was thinking about what Cole had just said or was off somewhere, far away. We were way away from town, way away from civilization, so the stars melded and swirled into patterns and designs of interlocking …

"Parabolas," I said, looking up myself.

"What?" Chevy said.

"Nothing. I was just thinking about Mrs. Hodges' class. Geometry. Sophomore year."

Chevy nodded, as if this was a logical thing to be thinking about.

"Long time ago," he said, once again looking up.

"Feels like it some nights," I agreed.

All of that shit, all of high school, seemed simultaneously like it was yesterday but then also like it was ancient history, 1,000 years ago. I wondered if that was what Einstein had meant when he had said time was relative. Or if it had even been Einstein who said that. Probably not. That was probably another part of high school I was remembering wrong.

"Bro," Cole said from where he was seated propped up against the ramp, "fucking untie me and let's fucking go. We all fucking know you're not going to do sh …"

And that was when Chevy stood up off the car hood, took two emphatic steps toward Cole, and put two in his head. Just like that. *WHAM*, wham. The second one sounding fainter because I wasn't wearing ear protection and the first one blew my hearing.

When it was done, Chevy went back to the truck and leaned up against it. He resumed his stance of staring up at the night sky. He looked like a man savoring a pleasure that he might not have access to for much longer.

"I guess you didn't need that potato after all," I said to him after a few minutes.

He scoffed. "I guess not. I forgot all about it, to be honest."

He continued to stare off into the night and, after a couple minutes, he said, "It's sure quiet now. Potato or no."

"Yeah," I agreed, not knowing what else to say. I wasn't worried he was going to kill me because I was a witness or anything. He wasn't like that. He wasn't some mad dog killer. He was just a guy with his heart broken, who was sick of the way things worked in our podunk little apple picking town.

"It's nice when it's quiet," he said. "We should have come out here more. All that neon and noise at the casino, at the bowling alley. Who fucking needs it."

It wasn't a question. The lights and the noise, the sound and the fury. Who fucking needs it.

Chevy didn't bother to dig the bullet out of the dirt, and we didn't bother to do anything with Cole's body, other than leaving it where it was sitting. It would have just been a waste of his last few precious hours of freedom. Maybe a waste of *our* last precious hours of freedom, depending on how the sheriff's department and the prosecutor decided to play it.

It took a couple of days for them to find the body. In that time Chevy could have run for Mexico or something, but instead he just enjoyed going about his regular life without having to see Cole's stupid face. I think that was all he had really wanted, at the end anyway. To do his little life without having somebody try to snatch his dignity away at every turn.

But they did eventually find the body, and when they did, they came looking for him straight and away. He didn't really confess to it, but he didn't really deny it either. If somebody were framing him they couldn't have done a much better job.

But this wasn't a mystery novel, wasn't *Law & Order*. Nobody framed him. He framed himself.

He got a life sentence, but could be up for parole after twenty. Word was that pissed off Cole's parents, but neither of them could sober up long enough to drive the bus on the prosecution or drum up popular outrage. The truth was that Cole didn't have that many friends in town. If he wasn't there to physically hand out money or drugs then there really wasn't any angle in sticking up for his memory. And so, nobody did.

So when Chevy gets out in twenty years—seventeen now, I guess, counting time served and the year since he's been in Walla Walla—what will he come back to? Cia got married to some other asshole from high school who didn't give a shit about any of that past drama. She's got a kid already with another on the way. Her folks love this new guy because he's wound a lot less tight than Chevy was.

When he comes back, he'll see that the orchards are all gone now. They tore them up to make room for vacation houses and wineries. They're trying to turn it into a Tuscany or Bourdeaux. They haven't made up their minds yet.

You hear a lot about the displacement of city people when they gentrify a downtown, but shit gets lost out here in the sticks, too. These little dramas that played out get plowed under. Paved over.

Maybe it's for the best. There's a lot of shit that happened out here that I'd rather not remember, anyway. Let them knock down the old processing plant, the high school with its old wrestling room, My Buddy's Place …

All that shit can go, as far as I'm concerned. Looking at it is just depressing as hell. Makes you want to shoot somebody. Possibly yourself.

CHRISTINE BOYER

WOMEN DO KNOW HOW TO CARRY ON

When Maddy woke, she thought she was dead.

It was dark. Quiet except for the wind and her own thudding heart.

Stupid, she thought. *If your heart's beating, you aren't dead.*

The dead don't feel pain either. Every nerve in Maddy jangled with pain. The twine binding her hands burned like hellfire on her wrists. Her head throbbed in time with her rabbity heartbeat. She managed to undo her hands and reached up, felt the sticky matting of blood in her hair. She felt the weeping edge of a wound just under her hairline.

Her mind blanked on what had happened. She knew all the stupid shit—her name, the year—but when she groped into the near-past, she found nothing.

Focus, she thought. *Move.*

She staggered to her knees, paused as nausea tore through her. Her skull felt too big, too heavy for her neck. She gathered up the grit and blood in her mouth and spit over and over until the iron tang faded.

She stood. Wavered. Her eyes adjusted to the darkness. It wasn't completely dark after all. Stars burned above her, and a warm yellow glowed in the distance. Some sign of civilization, a cluster of gas stations and restaurants that dot the interstate even in the most rural of places.

Maddy staggered toward that warm light. Across the field, over weed-choked hillocks pushed up by the cold. One shoe on, the other lost. She turned once to see where she woke up with her hands bound and her head split open: a ditch filled with fast-food wrappers, empty beer cans. Her would-be grave.

Thank Christ that Jules found her and not some piece of rough trade.

The girl stumbled out of the darkness like a damned ghoul. Filthy. Hard to tell what was dirt and what was blood. When Jules peered closer, she saw the girl had lost a shoe and left faint smears of blood with each step.

Jules ran across the parking lot as fast as she could. She caught the girl, braced for dead weight, but the girl was a wisp of nothingness, light as a curl of smoke. Jules's second thought was, *this girl needs fed up.*

Her first thought: *someone tried to kill this girl and failed, but just barely.*

She got the girl around the back of diner and into her trailer. That time of night, there was no one around but her anyway. Business didn't pick up until early morning when the overnight truckers left their sleeper cabins and rolled in for breakfast.

Inside, Jules surveyed the damage. A nasty gash on the head, a gnarl of bruised lump that had clotted shut. Rope burns around the wrists. Black eye. Torn fingernails, the nail beds oozing pink blood.

Worse injuries too. She peeled the girl out of her filthy clothes, eased her into a warm bath. The sight of a girl savaged by a monster in the night made Jules growl low in the back of her throat.

Jules got her into clean clothes and put her into her own bed. The girl came to her senses enough to talk. Gave her name, Maddy. Asked where she was.

"In my home," Jules replied. "I live behind the diner. Found you and brought you here."

The girl—Maddy—nodded. Seemed to remember. "You call the cops?" she asked.

"Got no local force. The state barracks are an hour away."

"You didn't call them?"

Jules scoffed. "Nope. They're worthless."

Maddy seemed relieved. She sagged back into the pillow with a hiss of pain. Jules guessed the reason: young girl dressed like that, found along the interstate. Probably had run-ins with the law, or at least a near miss or two.

She probably knew how police were. Life wasn't like a movie where some nice detective finds and arrests the bad guy. Maddy probably knew justice was a rare thing. Jules, an older woman, learned that lesson a long time ago…but she learned a more important lesson too: justice might be rare, but vengeance was entirely more accessible.

Jules kept watch over the girl.

She took the busy shift at the diner, bussed tables and kept the coffee carafes full. Checked in with her line cook. Stopped back to check on Maddy, who slept on her back with her mouth open, snoring.

A snore like that, loud as a bear—Jules figured the girl would be all right after all.

Back to the diner. Did the ordering for the week, the bookkeeping. Back to the trailer, took Maddy a lunch of toast and tea. Mild stuff for her stomach.

Back and forth. For a week, she handled her business and watched over the girl. Slept on the couch, felt her age in her back from sleeping all kinked up. Fed the girl, cleaned her wounds.

Jules always had a soft spot for strays. She had a small army of half-feral cats she fed out back. She got her line cook to winterize the old shed by the edge of the woods so the cats had shelter in bad weather.

Jack used to say she'd end up a crazy old cat lady smelling like piss, but Jules never saw any harm in that. Better to end up a cat lady because of a too-tender heart than end up bitter because the heart dried up, curled like a strip of old leather.

Maybe Maddy was just another stray for her to care for.

The bruises faded first. The rope burns scabbed over, left pink lines that faded to white. The torn fingernails grew back.

It took longest for her head to heal. The gash in her scalp healed slow and broke open easy. Jules probed at it each time, muttered that it could use stitches, but the thought of the hospital made Maddy's skin prickle with anxiety. The hospital meant cops, which meant questions, which meant hearing that it was her fault, what happened to her.

She'd heard that line before. It was nothing new, but it didn't mean she wanted to hear it again.

Maddy waited for the hammer to fall. Jules had to want something from her. People never helped for nothing, in Maddy's experience.

But Jules asked for nothing other than her own bed back, once Maddy's bruises faded.

"Couch is tough on my old bones," Jules said, and she looked apologetic.

"I should probably go anyway," Maddy replied, but she wasn't sure how to leave. She lost her wallet, her backpack. She had nothing.

"You don't have to," Jules said with a smile. "You just need to migrate on out to the couch."

"If I could stay until I pull together some cash…"

"I can hire you on at the diner. Keep it under the table, and you can keep any tips you make," Jules offered.

People never helped for nothing in Maddy's experience, but Jules seemed to be the exception.

Maddy stayed on through spring, and she seemed right as rain…except for whatever stalked her nightmares.

Even from the back bedroom, Jules could hear the girl's nightmares as she slept out on the couch. She whimpered, thrashed, woke up screaming in a glaze of sweat. She never went back to sleep afterwards—just sat out on the front steps with a cigarette and watched the sun rise. Sometimes Jules sat with her, her own cigarette smoldering between her fingers.

"You remember that night at all?" Jules asked.

The first time she asked, Maddy shook her head. Nope. No memory at all.

The second time, the girl hesitated before she said no.

After a bad spate of those beat-puppy-whimpering nightmares, Maddy muttered that she remembered some of it.

"Comes in flashes," she admitted. She flicked her cigarette, watched as a plug of ash tumbled into the scrubby grass. "I got a ride from him. Trucker."

"You were hitching?"

Maddy nodded. "From the city, going west."

"Heading to California?"

A shake of the head. "Nah. I was gonna find somewhere quiet to settle."

Jules snorted. "That's not usually how this sort of story goes, you know. Usually, it's a small-town girl moving to the big city."

"Guess I like to do things on the inverse."

Come summer, and the girl had some cash saved up but made no move to move on.

Jules didn't press the issue. She'd gotten used to the kid. Liked her company.

She worked hard at the diner. Jules always struggled to find good workers who stuck around—the local girls all aspired to bigger, better things in bigger, better places. Maddy stuck around: learned how to clean out the grease trap, how to take inventory, how to make the pies.

She didn't make the tips the other girls did. Her smile didn't come naturally to her. Jules didn't know if it was just her nature, how the good Lord made some people sour-looking, or if it was all the shit the world heaped on her at such a young age.

Sometimes the two of them sat outside at night, smoked and fussed over the cats that wound around their ankles. Maddy talked about her past sometimes, those nights. Growing up in the city. No father, shitty mother with her shitty boyfriends. How some of the boyfriends just leered at her, how others did worse. How she was always going to leave the city anyway, but all those shitty men made it easier to go.

Some small-town girls were destined for the energy of cities, the all-night places full of people and noise. Jules guessed that Maddy was the inverse, as she had said: big-city girl destined for a quieter life. Despite the nightmares, the girl seemed to find peace in the little town. More than once, Jules caught her outside late at night, head tilted back, gazing up at the stars like a loveable dope.

Jules knew why she didn't push the girl away. A better woman would have told her to git, to be gone. Maddy was young, and the whole world waited out there for her.

Jules knew the regret of a life spent in only one place. But she guessed that wouldn't be Maddy's regret. Barely eighteen, she'd already seen some of the world and all the misery in it.

Barely eighteen. Jules's own girl would have been about that age if…*if*. She'd lost the pregnancy too early to tell the sex. There had been nothing discernably human, just a rush of blood and pain, but Jules's always thought of it as a girl. Her daughter.

So maybe she didn't push Maddy away because she was living some mother-daughter fantasy. So what? They got along. Didn't squabble. Maddy worked hard at the diner, and Jules kept her fed with a roof over her head.

In autumn when the mornings were glazed with frost, they spent a weekend cleaning out the smaller second bedroom in the trailer. Jules used it for storage before, but it was time to clean it out, make space for better things.

"What's all this stuff?" Maddy asked. Jules glanced over, saw the girl with her nose curled at the piles of boxes.

"Jack's stuff. My husband."

Maddy poked through a box, pulled out a pair of battered gloves. Jules recognized them—Jack wore them for long rides with his buddies. "What happened to him?"

"He died."

Maddy winced. "Shit. Sorry, Jules."

"It's old news. Happened nearly twenty years back now," Jules replied with a shrug. "Used the life insurance to buy the diner. Sold his second bike to buy the empty lot next to it for truck parking. It was Jack's dream, actually—to buy the place and make it a bar."

"Why didn't you make it a bar then?"

Jules laughed. "Shit, it's hard enough dealing with truckers ornery from the road. I wouldn't want to deal with drunks every night."

Maddy offered a rare smile. "If anyone could handle them, it's you."

Jules returned the smile, turned back to the box she'd been sorting through. "I've had a lifetime of dealing with drunks. I'm glad to have that shit behind me, missy."

It wasn't the life Maddy imagined for herself, but it wasn't bad either.

She imagined her life as more picturesque—a lakeside cabin, not a double-wide behind a diner. She had a view, though: behind the trailer, across the span of scrubby grass and past the old tumbledown shed rose a forested ridge that washed in fiery gold each night when the sun set.

The trailer wasn't bad either. She had her own room, just a narrow space with a narrow bed, but it belonged to her. When she shut the door at night, no one busted in to press a hand over her mouth and hiss in her ear to be quiet.

She learned things in this new life too. Jules taught her how to make pies—real ones with homemade dough and fillings, nothing out of a can or freezer aisle. Maddy's pies were shitty at first, then mediocre, then pretty damned good. They earned Jules's approval, a nod and a pat to her back to show her pride.

Maybe it wasn't what she had imagined, but what woman ever got her dream life? She thought back to the girls she met on the road. Those girls with their dreams. The one who dreamt of Nashville, a lucky break away from writing heartbreak songs for steel guitars. The one on her way to Hollywood to be a star. They all had bigger dreams than her, but they all lived the same rough life on the road and never seemed to get any closer to those dreams.

Maddy's new life was quiet. No one bothered her. She worked, went home to the trailer. She went into town with Jules for groceries and got a new book from the library each trip. Another nice revelation: without the stress of her old home life or the ceaseless noise of the city, Maddy became a reader.

That's what made her life good enough, in the end. The last little thing. An honest job feeding people, a quiet place to sleep, and endless books to disappear into.

The only real shadow? *That* night.

She dreamt of it. Dreamt of waking in that ditch with every part of her hurting. Waking and seeing the stars and realizing she wasn't dead.

She remembered catching a ride with a trucker, looking to chew up mileage on the interstate instead of the fits and starts she'd been doing. A stupid mistake, reckless. Maddy wondered if she was alive because of her thick skull or if it was dumb luck.

As the memories returned, she relayed them to Jules, who nodded, took the information, and filed it away.

The memories of the man: cologne like astringent. A braided leather bracelet. Thick-lensed glasses set in heavy plastic frames.

She remembered more about the truck. The truck loomed large in her nightmares. She dreamt of the closed-in feeling of the cab, scrabbling for the door handle before a supernova of pain exploded in her head.

She remembered other details: a pine tree air freshener, the way the artificial scent mingled with the cologne. A placard of the Virgin Mary clipped to the sunscreen.

She wished she could forget it. Waking hours, she did—she pushed those memories so far to the back of her mind that she nearly forgot them altogether. The nightmares brought them back in vivid technicolor every night.

It was the dead of winter, less than a year later when Maddy's attacker pulled his rig into the diner parking lot.

Jules always guessed it could happen. She had put it together early on, the way her girl had come staggering out of the darkness that night. Maddy wasn't local, and who the hell else would have left her out there? Not a local boy—they got up to their own brand of trouble, drunk driving and hunting out of season and sometimes dabbling in drugs.

Jules also guessed the guy might return someday. The interstate ran less than a mile past them, and some truckers ran the same route, coast to coast, back and forth. In Jules's experience, truckers—like most people—were creatures of habit too. The same guys ordering the same skirt steak, the same slice of pie. Sit in the same booth to eat. Listen to the same songs on the juke box.

She'd kept an eye out for him. A guy with a leather bracelet, thick glasses. A guy who splashed on cologne with a heavy hand. The seasons changed, and they settled into the cold heart of winter, and Jules remained watchful.

And now he was here.

Maddy worked the counter that day, chatting with the few local codgers there when the guy walked in. Something must have sparked against her broken memories because she turned paper-white, set her coffee urn down, and disappeared into the back.

The guy didn't notice. Jules watched him as he settled into a booth, then went over to take his order. Thick glasses perched on his nose, made his eyes swim behind the lenses. A braided leather bracelet peeked out from the cuff of his shirt. The inside of Jules's nose stung at the miasma of cologne.

The truest proof came from Maddy herself: curled up on the office floor, knees to her chest. When Jules found her, the girl trembled with an animal fear that couldn't be faked.

The older woman knelt in front of her, cupped her face between her hands.

"Listen," she said, firm. "Are you listening?"

A long beat, but Maddy focused on her. Nodded.

"You ain't gonna get justice for this, you understand? Even if we went to the police back then, they wouldn't have done anything. This shit happens every day all over, and there's never justice for it."

Another nod. Maddy's eyes filled with tears.

"Women, we get kicked down, but we pick ourselves up, yeah? We get the shit end, but we keep going. We make our own way," Jules continued.

Maddy blinked against her tears. "I guess."

"We can get revenge." She said it slow, watched as the words hit the girl.

"I don't…what?"

"Do you want revenge on the man who hurt you and left you for dead?"

Maybe Maddy was her daughter in another life after all. She swiped at her tears with the back of her hand, but she gazed back at Jules with a coldness she never showed before. Then she nodded.

It went off without a hitch, but Jules wasn't sure if it was the perfect conditions coming together just so or karma—or just dumb luck.

The weather helped more than anything. Late afternoon, the weather turned ugly: frigid, pellets of icy snow whipped by the wind.

Perfect conditions. If the trucker had come through in the summer, it wouldn't have worked. Jules didn't think that quick to come up with a different plan.

The diner emptied out quick. The few locals saw the worsening weather, paid up, left. There were two truckers left—a young guy reading a trade magazine, and the monster. The former eyed the weather, and then paid and left too. The latter stayed, seemingly content to hunker down in his sleeper cab for the night.

Jules sent the line cook and the other waitress home, told them to drive safe. She sent Maddy to the trailer with instructions.

When Maddy returned, she palmed off the little bottle to Jules, who dumped it into a Styrofoam cup in the back, out of sight. Then she poured in some coffee, made a show of walking to his table and handing it off.

"Cold out there," she said, nodding at the window. "We're closing up on account of the storm, but take this to go. On the house."

He settled his bill, took the coffee. He even smiled when he thanked her, and it made Jules's stomach churn in disgust.

Maddy returned to the trailer while Jules locked up. She changed out of her uniform, locked herself in her room. She heard Jules come back not long after her, and then nothing else. When she pulled back the curtain in her window, she saw the truck sitting in the lot next to them. She knew he was tucked in his sleeper cabin, snug and warm—close enough that a spike of fear lanced through her.

The bottle of eye drops. When Jules promised revenge, Maddy's first dark thought was murder, not a cramped stomach or puking. Her hand drifted up to her hairline. She traced a fingertip along the ridge of scarring, remembered the way it throbbed for weeks after the attack.

The asshole deserved death, not a sour stomach. Maddy nodded off after a long while, and for the first time, her surrogate mother disappointed her.

Maddy woke early. The sky grew lighter in the east, but dawn was still an hour away. She got up, went to the bathroom, then peered out at the parking lot again. The truck was still there, crusted over in glittering ice from the winter storm that had raged all night.

She sighed. She padded into the kitchen and started the coffee. As it started to hiss and brew, she scrubbed her hands over her face and looked around. Near the front door sat Jules's boots, slumped over in a puddle of snowmelt.

The coffee pulled the older woman from her bedroom. She fixed Maddy with a studious gaze before she gestured at the kitchen table.

"Sit down. I'll get the coffee."

Maddy did as directed. Jules brought over mugs, then poured the coffee. She settled into the seat opposite and fixed Maddy with that gaze again.

"First thing first. We're opening the diner later this morning on account of the weather, but otherwise, today's just a normal day. Got it?"

Maddy nodded.

"Second thing. Cops'll be around. Answer their questions, short and direct. Don't get chatty with 'em."

"I don't understand. Why would there be cops?"

Jules blew along the surface of her coffee. "I'm gonna call them. In a day or two, depending."

"For what?" She shook her head, confused. "We just slipped him some eye drops."

"What do you think happens when someone drinks a whole bottle of them?"

"They get sick to their stomach."

Jules smiled but it didn't reach her eyes. "It ain't like in the movies. It's poison, pure and simple. Drops the blood pressure, makes a person sluggish." She glanced at Maddy. "Causes hypothermia."

A chill coursed down her spine. "He's dead? In his truck?"

Jules watched her for a long beat, obviously weighing what to tell her. "Not in his truck," she finally replied.

"Then where—"

"I went out after you fell asleep," Jules cut in. She nodded to where her boots sat in their puddle of melted snow. "I went out and knocked on his cab. I pretended to be checking on him in the storm."

Maddy gaped at her. Said nothing.

"I wasn't sure if he'd drink the coffee or not, you know. But he did. He was sick. Sluggish. He seemed drunk. I convinced him to leave the truck. Told him I'd take him somewhere warmer."

"You brought him here?"

She shook her head. "No. I led him into the woods behind us. I took him up to the ridge, got him all turned around, and left him."

Maddy took in her words. "It was really cold last night..." she started.

"...and he was already hypothermic," Jules finished. "I went back to his truck and got the empty coffee cup. And this."

She reached into the pocket of her frayed sweatshirt. She pulled something out and slid it across the table. Maddy plucked it between her fingertips and turned it over: the Virgin Mary placard. The one tucked into the sunscreen of her nightmare truck.

She should have felt horrified. Or guilty. Maybe he had family, a wife and kids. She reached up and touched the ridge of scarring on her head. Any horror or guilt remained out of reach, though she didn't reach very hard for it.

"So, he's dead?" she asked.

"Maybe. Maybe he found his way back to his truck." Jules arched an eyebrow at her. "Maybe he saw the light of the diner through the trees and made his way to safety, like he left you to do."

They opened the diner late that morning.

Few customers turned up anyway. Part of the interstate closed after a pile-up. The county trucks worked overtime to scrape and salt the roads.

Late afternoon, Jules gazed out the diner windows and said, casual, "there's still a truck parked from overnight."

The couple of locals at the counter heard her, but didn't reply.

Two days after, Jules called the cops on the non-emergency line. She pulled on a persona Maddy never heard before: the dumb old broad. The needless worrier.

"I don't want to make a big deal of it," she heard Jules say. "But the truck's been here a few days. I went to check it out, but there was no one there."

Karma or dumb luck—Jules didn't care either way.

A couple of staties made the drive out. They poked around the abandoned truck, asked some questions. They asked

Maddy, who shrugged and said she hadn't seen the guy since the night of the storm.

They took notes. They thanked Jules and left.

The locals, usually bereft of any real scandal, speculated. There was chatter of drug running or human trafficking. The interstate ran from coast to coast and truckers were thick on the road. Impossible to police all of them. It'd be easy for an independent contractor to run drugs or women, then fall into bad trouble in that seedy underworld.

A pair of hunters found the body during spring gobbler season. When she had left him, he had been curled against a tree. She'd left that part out in the retelling to Maddy: how she had stood shivering in the weather and watched him die.

The elements and the wildlife had made neat work of the monster, leaving little beyond scraps of clothing and scattered bones.

"Best we can figure, he left his truck during the storm and wandered away. Got lost in the woods, froze to death," the state detective told Jules.

"Flatlanders," she replied with a sad shake of her head.

She heard through the local gossip channels that the state investigator ruled it as death by misadventure. It became a cautionary tale about taking the weather in these parts seriously.

The police gathered the bones they could find. The truck had already been towed away months before the hunters found the body.

Maddy's nightmares seemed to disappear. Jules didn't hear the beat-puppy whimpering through the thin walls anymore. The girl put on weight too, rounded out the sharp edges of her frame and got some meat on her.

They only ever talked about it once. After the cops came and went, after the truck and bones were taken away, Maddy only brought it up the once.

The two of them sat outside. The summer was muggy, but the evenings cooled off nice with the breeze off the ridge. Maddy sighed, content, and took a sip of her longneck.

"How'd you know it'd all come together?" she asked. Jules cast her a sidelong glance, then lifted her shoulder in a half-shrug.

"Didn't. It was a lucky confluence of circumstances."

"*Confluence*, huh? There's a ten-dollar word."

"You ain't the only one who reads, missy." Maddy heard the smile in Jules's voice, smiled in reply.

"I like to think it was karma," Jules continued. "The whole time you were healing up, I was thinking. A man like that, you weren't his first. I think the world can't abide good and bad being off balance for too long. A man like that? It's like a thumb on the scale. Maybe that lucky confluence was the balance righting itself."

Maddy eased a thumbnail under the label of her beer bottle. "That's pretty deep."

"I don't consider it murder. We didn't shoot the fucker. We didn't slash his throat. We leaned into the circumstances presented to us and karma tipped it the rest of the way."

Maddy nodded. It sounded like what her guidance counselor used to call *twisting the truth*, but Maddy guessed her guidance counselor was never left to die in a ditch.

"Anyway, I seen it before." Jules took a sip of her own beer.

"Seriously?"

Jules grunted out the affirmative. Added, "My old man. Jack."

Maddy opened her mouth to laugh, but Jules's tone wasn't a joking one.

"You serious?" she asked instead.

"Maybe." A long beat, and then she added, "Maybe Jack was a mean drunk and blew his paycheck every week on his bikes and booze. Maybe he was a cliché. Maybe he went on a bender and did something that couldn't be undone."

Maddy swallowed hard. "What'd he do?"

"Put me in the hospital. But it wasn't just me he hurt. I lost the baby. I told everyone I fell, lied for that fucker when he was the one that stomped me. I get discharged, and maybe he didn't seem quite contrite enough. For murdering our girl."

"And you…" She couldn't finish the sentence.

"Maybe I just leaned into the circumstances one night. Jack got liquored up all the time. Maybe that night, I riled him up to keep drinking, then convinced him to get on that motorcycle with no helmet. Sent him off into the night."

Maddy was silent for a moment, then added, "and karma did the rest."

"Seems like it did. Took a turn too fast and went headfirst into a tree."

Maddy didn't reply, and Jules didn't offer any more. They never talked about their other shared secret again either, the confluence of circumstances that led to one less monster walking in the world.

They just sat together in comfortable silence, drinking their beers and watching the fireflies flicker like low-hovering stars. Just two women who kept going, who keep going—making their own way.

Mildred could see the man's life had left him.
She'd split a lot of firewood.

Russell Thayer

SOMEWHERE BETWEEN RAGGED AND RIGHT

On the east side of the cold valley, a failing sun dressed rough peaks in pink satin. Shadows haunted the west side, where Mildred ran up worn porch steps, burst into the farmhouse, then hurried to her bedroom at the end of a dim hallway. She began to fill a duffel bag her father brought back from the war. Socks. Sweater. Hairbrush. Clean underthings. Tin of hard candy. Framed picture of her dead mother. Torn nightgown. Her stepfather's Model 10 revolver, missing two rounds.

Looting the coffee can in the kitchen, Mildred shoved twenty-two dollars into the pocket of her blue jeans. Flames bloomed around the frame of the barn. A horse with frantic eyes trotted past the kitchen window. Her mother's horse. She'd chased it from its stall before closing the doors on her stepfather.

Ragged brown hair hung to her shoulders, hiding bruises from the night before. Her own bedroom. She'd been expecting him since the day her mother went into the ground.

She should have run to a new life straight from the graveyard. A half hour ago, he'd come after her again, in the barn, saying he'd blow her brains out if she didn't get on her knees and let him mount her like a prize bull. He'd slapped her when she spit in his boozy face. Then Bristol, her loyal cattle dog, charged at the man as he pulled the Model 10 from the waist of his britches. One round soon missing. Bristol dead. He'd set the pistol on a hay bale as he worked the buckle of his belt. His last mistake.

Sinking into the family rocker, Mildred pulled on heavy boots, tugging the laces so hard her fingers burned. Standing, she drew a wool jacket around her shoulders, grabbed a knitted hat, scarf, and mittens. Stopping at the door of her hollow home for one last look, the calendar caught her eye. March 1934. She'd be eighteen in three weeks.

Two hours later, a mile west of Wallace, Idaho, Mildred tramped in blue moonlight down a trail to the edge of Highway 10. She'd have to stay away from lawmen. Find a job. Out of state. Spokane. Maybe Ellensburg. She thought about what she'd left behind. Bristol gone. No family. She didn't make friends easily. Girls at school scolded her for not bathing. She wore shabby clothes to parties. Sulked. Got into fights.

Standing in the road on two strong feet, the strap of the duffel bag biting into her shoulder, Mildred looked east toward Montana, then west toward the Pacific. At age eleven, her mother had taken her to Seattle by train, before her father died and her stepfather had come along to ruin their lives. City living remained a dream for Mildred after their return. Then her mother fell down a flight of stairs at home a month ago, old bruises fading on her shattered skull, and everything had become a nightmare. Mildred turned toward Spokane, the gravel crunching under her feet. Clouds now hid the moon.

The rumble of a truck grew behind her. Her mother had warned her to stay away from the big rigs growling through the panhandle. Snow started to fall.

The machine rolled to a stop. The driver's door squeaked, and Mildred could hear boots scrape as he came around the front of the truck. He looked older than her stepfather. Rawboned. Ugly. He wore a cowboy hat and she guessed he hadn't shaved for a week. Stroking a droopy gray mustache, he looked around at the shadows, maybe fearing an ambush.

"It ain't safe alone out here," he said. "Get in the cab. It's warm inside."

She could die in there or die out here. Nobody would care.

He helped her up. She set the bag between her legs, the pistol within reach.

"Where you headed on a night like this?" the driver asked as he took the wheel.

"Spokane."

"Why ain't you on the train? Does your pappy know you're out here by yourself?"

"I need work."

"Jobs is hard to come by these days. I'm headed to Seattle. Gonna stop in Kellogg for the night. You're welcome to sleep in the cab."

Mildred nodded. The smell of the man's unwashed clothes hadn't turned her stomach yet.

"Got any money?" he asked.

"No."

"I'll get you breakfast."

"Thanks," she said, taking off her hat.

"You're sure pretty."

A humming started in her ears, and Mildred looked out the window as the truck ground forward, gaining speed. She knew she was good-looking. She'd known it since grown men started staring at her with their mouths open. Lingering looks that made her skin twitch. A handsome neighbor she sometimes worked for kissed her one afternoon before she turned sixteen. A thrill had gone through her like his tongue. He'd gripped her breasts and panted in her ear and she felt like she'd been shot to the moon. Nothing more had come of the kiss, but she stopped going around to the neighbor's house. After that, she found herself in a man's headlights every time she left her room. Even when she stopped bathing.

In Kellogg, the driver came to rest at a truck stop. Mildred used the grimy bathroom. A weary girl leaned against the sink, washing herself with wet paper towels. She hadn't been born pretty, but had what men wanted, and looked at Mildred with dull eyes and yellow teeth.

When Mildred returned to the truck, the driver handed her a hamburger wrapped in paper. She ate quickly, wondering if he'd ask her to pay for her food the way the girl in the bathroom made her way. The moment came after she'd settled onto her end of the bench with a blanket.

"How's about a kiss before bed?" he asked as he crushed a cigarette in the ashtray.

Her skin tensed. A sound like rustling cattle grew in her head.

"Just one," she said, knowing there would be more. "I'm tired."

"Sure," he said. "Just one."

Mildred crawled toward the trucker on shaking arms and planted her lips on his rough cheek. As she turned back to her spot, he grabbed her neck and pushed her face down toward his lap. She watched up close as he unbuckled his belt. Girls talked about this sort of thing at school. Laughed about it. Lived in fear of it. She wanted to run, but the truck would let her run faster. Closing her eyes, she imagined herself in a sunny meadow, Bristol at her side.

"Don't be shy, boys. She's eager for it. And cute as a button."

Mildred opened her eyes to the words. She pulled the blanket tight around her neck, hoping the trucker would stop jawing with his friends outside and start the engine so she could get warm.

"We're movin' on to Seattle," the driver continued. "Don't think too long about it. You won't find a tastier grouse between here and Chicago." Wind muffled his voice, but Mildred began to understand.

"Five bucks, though?" said another man. "These are hard times, Mac. Give a guy a break."

"Nope. She's worth five. Tell your friends. We'll be here all mornin'."

"Let me have a look at her."

"Nope. Five. Up front. Trust me."

Mildred's heart began to thump. Could travelling this way be better than the sheriff finding her?

The driver's door opened and a man climbed in. Before Mildred could cover her face with the blanket, she noted his heavy belly and dirty clothes. He pulled the blanket away and looked down at her with an open-mouthed smile as he motioned at her to get her pants off. Seattle's just a day away, she told herself, finding the meadow again, and Bristol's soft ears.

After the man left, Mildred shivered under the blanket. In ten minutes, another man came for her. Then one more after that.

"How you doin' in there?" asked the driver through the open door as the third man left. He tossed her his handkerchief.

"Are we about square?" Mildred asked as she wiped herself. "For a lift and a lousy hamburger?" Blood stained the fabric. Her cycle couldn't have come at a better time.

"I guess," he said. "Don't see nobody else linin' up."

After a few minutes, the driver climbed in with a bag of warm burgers, and they set out west toward Spokane.

"You're a desperate thing," he said as the truck bounced along. "That's what I figured when I saw you alone on the shoulder last night with all your gear and no cash."

"I still got no cash." She'd hidden the twenty-two dollars in her sock.

"Don't worry 'bout that. You'll make us plenty in Spokane once I get you in a dress. I'm Hubert, by the way."

Mildred hated her name, and planned to never say it out loud again.

"My gunsel girl got no name?" he asked.

She stared out the window as they rolled through Coeur d'Alene, the fresh debt of another hamburger heavy in her belly.

At a rest area near the state line, Hubert pulled the truck into a pocket of trees. He hopped to the ground and trotted off to the outhouse. Mildred used the break to search in the duffel bag for her stepfather's big pistol. It held a .38 cartridge, and she thought she'd like to blow Hubert's whole head off.

The pistol had disappeared. With a flurry of anger, Mildred scrambled around the cluttered cab looking for it. It wasn't in the glove compartment or behind the seat with all the other tools. He must have it on him.

She tucked a large wrench under the bench when she spotted him walking back to the truck.

He climbed up to his spot at the wheel and lit a cigarette. Mildred cracked the window.

"Thinkin' I might take a nap," said Hubert, "Maybe after a kiss."

"Jesus Christ," said Mildred.

"Come on, girl. I'm takin' you to Seattle."

"And I'm much obliged."

"That ain't worth a thing these days."

"Why is this?" she asked, grabbing her crotch. He stared at her as if he thought her a damn fool.

"You could walk," he said.

"I'm on my cycle down there."

"Good for you. Your female blood don't mean a thing to me."

Mildred looked at the trees through the glass as he arranged her on the bench, removing her boots and blue jeans.

"You stink like a sardine can, but you're cuter'n Clara Bow. You can bank on that."

"If I ever get paid."

"You'll do all right. A girl looks like you."

Mildred figured it might be the worst thing that ever happened to her. Being born pretty. But she knew even an ugly girl could be in the same hard spot.

Hubert tossed his hat behind the seat. Thin white hairs on his dry scalp stuck up in all directions. After pulling his pants to his knees, he got between her legs and began to push hard into the mat of dark hair. When he groaned and collapsed against her chest, Mildred reached under the bench with her right hand and pulled out the heavy wrench. As he opened his eyes and tried to kiss her, she hit him repeatedly on the side of his head until he crumpled into a tangle with his trousers on the floor of the truck. After a few crushing whacks on his forehead, Mildred could see the man's life had left him. She'd split a lot of firewood.

A box behind the seat contained a pile of greasy rags. Mildred wiped blood off Hubert's face the best she could and strained to prop him up at the wheel. After trying to close his eyes with two fingers, she plopped the cowboy hat on his head, then fished the fifteen dollars she'd earned out of his billfold. A few seconds later she took the other twenty he carried. The first time she'd ever stolen anything from a stranger.

After searching Hubert's clothes, she dug around up under the dashboard and seat, but still couldn't find the pistol. He must have sold it at the truck stop in Kellogg.

Once she buttoned her jacket and pulled the knitted hat over her hair, Mildred dropped to the dirt with her bag and walked in a light snow out to the highway.

Cold chocolate passed through a paper straw at a soda fountain in the quiet Spokane bus station. The duffel bag sat on the floor at Mildred's feet. A chatty woman had picked her up on Highway 10, admonishing her about walking the road on her own, before dropping her in the city and making the girl promise to purchase a ticket for the trip to Seattle. The woman had even given her five dollars toward the fare. Mildred felt the wad of money thriving in her pocket, and planned to buy a chicken dinner before deciding on the train or bus. Or maybe she'd look for work right here in Spokane.

"That's a yummy-looking milkshake," said a mellow voice.

Mildred looked at the man. He possessed a full head of blond hair and ruddy cheeks.

"You're not getting any," she said. The fan of greasy hair that partly covered her face didn't seem to be working as a blind.

"I was thinking about ordering one myself," he said with a smile.

"Go ahead."

"What's your name?" he asked.

"I forget."

"You got amnesia? Want me to call a doctor?"

"A head-peeper, maybe."

"Nah. You seem like a regular girl."

Mildred looked at herself in the mirror behind the soda counter.

"Well, I'm gonna call you Vivian," he continued. "It has an elegant sound and I like to say it. I like the way it buzzes in my head." He paused, roll-tapping his fingers on the counter. "In fact, everything about you buzzes in my head."

"Okey-dokey." She licked the bottom of the straw.

"I'm Osgood Davis, in case you're interested."

"I'm not."

Osgood chuckled, then ordered a vanilla shake when the soda jerk came by. He slipped onto the stool next to Mildred. She could feel him surveying her dirty hair and grimy face. The bag at her feet.

"I peddle women's clothing to luxury shops," he said. "I carry a premium line from New York City." He felt around in his pockets. "Sometimes I stop at a bus station to see if someone might be interested in traveling along with me on my route. Saves them a ticket. Saves me falling asleep at the wheel." He lit a cigarette. "Gets lonely on the road. I like conversation."

"You just wanna stick your hambone in my beaver," said Mildred. She took a long suck on the straw. They were alone at the counter.

"That's not true," said Osgood after a startled pause. "Plenty of times I travel with men. I'm headed to Seattle after Yakima. Then Portland, San Francisco, Los Angeles. You heading to any of those places?"

"I'd head to your room, if you've got one. I'd like to clean up."

"Sure," said Osgood, rubbing his hands together.

Mildred studied the slender dress salesman, looking for danger, but couldn't find any meanness in his face.

They stopped at a motor court outside of town. After a long soak, Mildred twisted her wet hair up in a towel and stood in the bathroom doorway. A second towel covered her torso. Osgood lay on the bed, arms behind his head, and watched her tall frame move around. The smile he wore said a lot.

"You're not getting anything until I'm served dinner in a swell restaurant," said Mildred.

"Can I have a peek at dessert?" asked Osgood.

Five men had been at her the last two days. Mildred let the towel fall to the floor. She ripped the other towel from her head and shook out her hair.

Osgood's face lit up like a big-city movie marquee.

"Holy hell, Vivian. I say we hit the country club. And I've got just the thing for you to slink around in."

After Osgood bolted from the cabin, Mildred captured her flesh in a clean bra and step-ins from her bag. She'd purchased a box of sanitary napkins at the bus station. As she dug around for her hairbrush, Osgood reentered the cabin and laid a garment bag on the bed, unzipping it to expose a stack of dresses. He gently removed them one by one and hung them in the closet.

"You're just the right size," he said, shuffling through the samples. He pulled out a sheer, coral-colored number with a tulip skirt. He laid it on the bed and ran outside again. Mildred took a cigarette from his pack and lit it with his platinum lighter. She'd tried smoking a few times behind the high school with boys who were frightened to death of her.

She hadn't liked the hot smoke in her lungs, but these days everything deserved another chance.

Osgood returned with a suitcase and set it on the bed. He opened it and rummaged through the fabric, pulling out a slip.

"Leave your briefs on, but take off the bra. Let those beauties swing free. You'll knock 'em dead." He looked at her feet. "Throw your boots on. We'll get to a shoe store before dinner. I've got an all-wool crepe swing coat in the car that should fit you just fine."

Admiring her new two-tone oxfords, Mildred took another sip of wine. Osgood had bought her silk stockings, as well, and thanks to the end of Prohibition, she'd been served an alcoholic drink for the first time. She thought she might grow to love the sharp red nectar swirling in her bulbous glass. No one questioned Mildred's age when they ordered, but everyone looked at her in the fine dress. The softest fabric and brightest color she'd ever worn. Osgood had showered and shaved. Not a bad-looking fellow, she thought, though grey hair could be seen at his temples. The plight of the last few days began to ease under his generous attention.

"If we hit it off later, and you wanna join me on the road, I plan to dress you up in a different outfit every day and bring you with me to help entice my buyers. We'll make a killing in orders. You could start modeling in Los Angeles once we get there in two weeks. I know a few shops that would hire you in a minute."

"Where do women get the money to buy new things these days?"

"From husbands who could ride out the stock market crash" said Osgood, "Or from other men."

Mildred felt sick when they returned to the motel, her temples aching from the seductive wine. She vomited her meal into the toilet before staggering to bed. She took off her dress and sat on the edge of the mattress, her face in her hands.

"I don't want to," she said.

"You're not used to all that wine." said Osgood, putting his hand on her shoulder.

Mildred shook her head. Her eyes felt as big as eggs. The bed springs squeaked as Osgood got up. He brought her a glass of water and two aspirin.

Mildred felt better at dawn and took off her underthings for him. She didn't think of mountain meadows while he kissed her breasts. Osgood proved gentle and it didn't hurt when he pushed inside. She could tell by his culmination that he'd gotten his money's worth.

After a bath, at Osgood's request, Mildred shaved her armpits with his safety razor. He chose a light blue dress to put on over the silk stockings and Cuban-heeled oxfords. After coffee and eggs, the pair called on a shop in downtown Spokane. The owner nodded with appreciation as Mildred modeled various outfits, complimenting the young woman on her grace and appearance. Osgood beamed, and the woman winked at him while placing a large order.

At dinner that evening, Osgood reached around a flickering candle to take her hand.

"Will you come with me to Yakima tomorrow? I'll pay for everything on the road, and I'll give you two dollars a day to add to that roll you keep in your pocket."

Mildred remembered the smell of the truck, the five-dollar fee, and took a sip of wine.

"It's for the modeling, Vivian. You're gonna make me rich with commissions."

"Do you have a wife?" Mildred asked. He wore a ring.

"Not much of one."

"Do you have children?"

"No. We never could."

After another sip of wine, Mildred squeezed his hand.

On the twenty-eighth of March, outside of Modesto, Mildred revealed to Osgood the news of her birthday. When asked her age, she said she didn't remember. He laughed as they unloaded the samples into their cabin, then drove them down the highway to a roadhouse, babbling happily about how good she'd been for business in Seattle and Portland, spouting optimism about the success they'd have turning west to San Francisco and then south to Los Angeles. He kissed her hand before she got out of the car, and Mildred decided she didn't mind so much being pretty. She'd grown fond of Osgood's good humor and attention. He had a raw need for her that came every night, but she'd begun to enjoy the grappling.

As Osgood surveyed the menu, Mildred sipped wine and noticed two men enter the restaurant. She'd seen them drinking beer outside a cabin at the motor court. They settled at the bar. She could sense a hunger as they perched on their stools like broad-winged hawks.

After a large meal, and much wine, Mildred clapped her hands together when the waitress brought her a piece of chocolate cake. Sly Osgood must have informed the establishment of the special occasion when he visited the bathroom. He ordered her another glass of wine, but Mildred told the waitress to make it coffee instead.

"Yes, ma'am," said the woman, scribbling on her pad before tearing off the check and leaving it on the table. Mildred tasted the cake and watched Osgood take out his money. She wished he didn't carry so much. The fat billfold contained banknotes recently wired from New York for expenses on the road, and it didn't surprise her, when she turned her head, to see the two men at the bar sizing up the situation. They paid for their beers and departed. Their leaving didn't quell her growing anxiety.

As they walked to the car, Mildred ordered Osgood into the passenger seat. She felt like driving on her birthday. The power of his green Model A roadster excited her. As she backed out of the roadhouse parking lot, Osgood nodded off. Her eyes watched the road behind.

At the cabin, Mildred hurried a stumbling Osgood inside. After locking the door, she turned to find the two men coming out of the bathroom. She'd left the window open to air the room after her morning soak.

One of the men took Mildred's arm and pulled her toward the bed. Throwing her down, he pressed his knee into her spine. The other mug pushed Osgood around, grabbing the billfold from his shaking hand. He held a long knife. The man crushing her back moved rough fingers through her hair.

"Are we gonna take a little out of her before we go?" he asked his friend.

"That's an idea."

At that moment Osgood rushed to Mildred's defense, but the man blocked him easily and drove his long knife into Osgood's stomach twice with quick motions, holding Osgood's arm near the shoulder as he slumped to the floor.

"God damn it, Parnell," said the man on Mildred's back.

"He came at me."

Osgood groaned, trying to lift his head. Mildred struggled to get out from under the knee, and the brute soon lifted her by her arms and dragged her into the bathroom.

He tried to rip the dress off her back, and they were soon

thrashing in front of the sink. Mildred wrenched an arm free and drove the man backwards over the rim of the clawfoot tub, where he knocked his skull hard against the porcelain. Gaining her balance, she grabbed his head and beat it against the rim until blood began to flow. As the door behind her came open, a stained blade leading the way, Mildred spun to the floor and kicked it shut with her sturdy oxfords, knocking the knife from the intruder's hand. While she pressed the door against the arm, her back against the tub, she picked up the knife and slashed the underside of his wrist, blood pouring onto the tile. The man screamed, heaving himself against the blocked door in an effort free his arm. Mildred took her weight away just as his momentum carried him into the tight room, where he fell on top of her, the knife penetrating deep under his ribcage. As he rolled onto his back, wheezing and gurgling, she extracted the blade and severed the cartilage in his throat. The motions reminded Mildred of the times she'd helped her father field-dress an elk. She was good at it. The cutting felt right.

After performing the same procedure on the second man, she scrambled on hands and knees to Osgood's side, slipping in his blood as she frantically clutched his lifeless head.

"Osgood. My dear Osgood," Mildred whispered, soon in tears. It felt like the first time she'd ever wept.

Stepping over lifeless limbs in the bathroom, Mildred scrubbed the blood from her arms and face with a wet washcloth. She then covered Osgood with a quilt, emptied the wallets of all three men, and quietly moved the garment bags and clothing to the roadster.

Mildred paused in Bakersfield for gasoline. Once she hit Los Angeles, she stopped in a shady parking lot to sleep. Later, she found her way to a bungalow court on West Sunset Boulevard, registering as Vivian Davis. She paid for one night. That left $112 in her roll. After a bath, she brushed her hair, put on the coral-colored tulip dress, her oxfords, and walked out to the boulevard. She didn't need a wrap in the evening air, and the sense of that opened her eyes to the world around her. Imagine being warm at night, she thought as she walked past fragrant oleander. She soon found herself in front of Hollywood High. As she spun in a circle, her arm around a palm trunk, she wondered what her schoolmates at Wallace High thought of her now. After staring at the vacant classroom windows, Mildred strolled up North Orange Drive, toward Hollywood Boulevard. In a fancy hotel, the bar lit with warm light, she met a man and went to his room with him. He called her gorgeous and gave her $15 dollars to let him do the things he most desired. She pretended to like it.

Back at the bungalow, Mildred sipped wine in the kitchenette and pondered the transaction. Hotel work wouldn't be like her time in the truck. And now $127 lay tight under the rubber band. She didn't think she'd like to visit a stranger's room every night, but she knew she could if she had to. She'd never worked a regular job. She knew how to butcher animals. She'd learned how to make an impression in well-designed clothing. Osgood had suggested she look for modeling work. Brushing her hair in the bathroom mirror before bed, Mildred decided she might even hire a taxi to take her to a moving-picture studio. To find out how beautiful she really was.

In the morning, Mildred studied the little tourist map she'd taken from the hotel office and drove to Griffith Park. At an overlook, she surveyed the basin below. Hollywood lay to the south, the vast Pacific Ocean sparkling in the distance. Construction had begun on a large astronomical observatory. She strolled around the foundation. A man wearing a soiled undershirt whistled at her as he unloaded a truck. Returning to the roadster, Mildred pulled out one of Osgood's large suitcases. She'd filled it with her favorite dresses and all the underthings she'd need for now. She'd forgotten the framed picture of her mother back at the motor court in Modesto, inside the duffel bag with the rest of her threadbare Idaho life. She should have burned everything that belonged to her, but she knew the wind would cover her tracks before long. Done with her name, done with woeful Mildred, she lowered the roadster's convertible top and dropped Osgood's keys on the seat where anyone could see them. It felt right to leave a gift during hard times.

Strolling across the warm parking lot, suitcase in hand, Vivian imagined herself a fresh young woman, new to the big city, with a look and a name that buzzed. She felt a rumble in the earth under her feet, a fault-line waking up. With that as a sign of affirmation, she increased her step, chin high, and disappeared into the world.

MATT PHILLIPS

BLACK ROSE

1

The way I come up, way out here where there's nothing, mama tells us white boys, "Don't you never touch that black ink, baby. It'll get you put to hell faster than a bullet does a mean dog." We take that to heart, us white boys. There ain't nothing like a sexy black girl to make a white boy fidget, take his hands out of his pockets. You get caught flicking your pud when a black girl walks by, you got buddies known you since duck-height lining up to roast your ass.

Kind of funny that way, racial relations.

Me, I'm just a poor white boy came up in a Jesus Christ Is Our Savior kind of house. My mama feared nothing more than she feared the lightning strike of Almighty Christ His Lord. I myself think the lighting strike happens to be a little more metaphorical, as the sidewalk preachers call it. Like a story to help you stay true to the Lord. Do wrong, they say, and he's gonna get you one way or another. Strike you down, one way or another.

There's all kinds of sins in this life. What confuses white boys like me is that sometimes a sin is all there is—only sins as choices. You got a buddy, he gets caught loving on a black girl, you beat his ass straight into the dirt. Some say it's a sin to harm your brother. But there's a bigger sin in that story that calls for reckoning. See how that works? I always say it that sins against race got more weight than all other sins. Again, my experience. Maybe it shouldn't be that way, but it's damn clear to me—that's how it fucking is.

I can tell you how it is in a podunk town like mine:

If rumors come at you, some hick says he saw you kissing a black girl at the movies or under the stars out by Font's Point, that stain don't never leave you alone. Again, my experience. Even trashy white girls won't give you the charity hand treatment, they hear you been taking pleasure with a black girl. I know there's some of you think to call me a race baiter, say I was born racist and there ain't nothing I can do to disprove that. And maybe you're right. Could damn well be.

But I got to tell you to listen to my whole story. It ain't what you think.

See, all those things your mama tells you, all the times your daddy took his belt to you, all the whispers about Jesus Christ Our Lord, they can't hold a skinny pole to the power of love. No, sir. No, they cannot. You remember love, don't you? My experience, see, it's people get older and they forget what it's like—how it is to see a girl and fall right into her, plunge in cold like we did out at the quarry when we was teenagers. You get old, you get so you need everything to be same-looking, all regular and what you expect. Take the church: We got black churches and we got white churches. So people see what they expect and not a damn thing more. We don't mix without it meaning something, and I don't mean anything bad about His Lord by this.

It's the way it is. And it ain't the way it ain't.

I don't mind saying I'm a white boy all the way through,

but I won't say I ain't got a bone for love in me. Shit. Sometimes love is all there is. Hang on now and listen. I need me some of that brown liquor before I get into it. You know what they say about that brown liquor—has just enough devil in it to keep you dancing around the lightning.

2

The wife didn't like me working nights. Me, I liked night shifts. Just me and the quiet stocking shelves for eight hours. The wife used to say she missed me in bed, but it was a goddamn lie. She didn't miss fuck-all—I knew my wife since we were toddlers, and I swear to the Good Lord himself that she never told it true when she could find fun in a lie. The wife was getting whatever she wanted. I can give you more on that later, but the point here is to tell you about the night shifts. Because the night shifts is how me and Diedra met.

I was killing time in my pickup before punching in, listening to an old Jerry Jeff Walker tape, and Diedra parked her t-top Trans Am next to me. This vehicle was loud. I expected to see some jackass driving—maybe a Macho Man Randy Savage lookalike—but instead I saw a black woman with tied up hair, all crinkled into a bun, and a pair of lips that painted their own profile. I mean that in a damn good way. Lips you wanted to pinch with your teeth. My learned nature caught up with me and I reminded myself: That's a black girl you're looking at, white boy.

She got out of the Trans and rapped her knuckles on my passenger side window. I leaned over and rolled it down for her. "Yeah?"

"You got Jerry Jeff on the radio?" She had a voice that made her questions come out as compliments. "Jerry Jeff Walker?"

"It's a tape," I said.

"Look at you—even got Jerry Jeff on a tape." She put one hand to a cheek and tilted her head at me. "It's my first night. They mind we clock in early five or ten minutes?"

"They mind," I said. "They mind we clock in thirty seconds early."

"You're saying we work for assholes."

I smiled and shrugged, rubbed the back of my neck. "I'm saying asshole don't begin to cover it."

Diedra yawned and shook her head. "Makes you tired, don't it?" she said. "These assholes in charge of it all. Acting like anything matters outside a good fuck and a drink."

Did I say this is a love at first sight story? Well, it is.

But that don't begin to cover it.

3

That was how it started, but it really got cooking with a touch.

Both of us—me and Diedra—were throwing bags of dog chow onto the second shelf of a custom-built endcap. The dog food sales guy had a cardboard dog bigger than a Dodge Powerwagon framing the whole thing and it wobbled each time we tossed a bag onto it. I said, "This puppy looks drunk." And Diedra laughed, but when she threw the next bag onto the shelf, that damn dog lunged right toward her—this big old retriever coming down on her like golden cloud blown down by God Himself. I grabbed her around the waist and spun the both of us away out into the aisle. We watched the thing crumple and fall apart, all the bags of dog food crunching against each other. I heard Rick Eber cuss a few aisles over—that same supervisor tone we all know in his voice—and it took a minute before I realized: Me and Diedra were staring at the downed dog, and she had her ass right in my business. I had my hands draped across her belly and there was some kind of blood flow starting up for both of us. By the time Rick and the crew came around to help us pick up, me and Diedra pried ourselves apart, but I knew then we were stuck together.

They say different color ink don't mix. But I'm a stone-cold white boy raised up in the old ways, and I can tell you for a damn fact: If we don't mix, we sure do swirl. And sometimes a swirl is better than a whole new color.

4

We got together for the first time—I'm talking about naked bodies now—it was like smashing a beer bottle into concrete. It shattered the both of us. I never saw a black girl naked before, and I want to say it's different. But it's no different—darker maybe, but just as plush and beautiful as you ever seen it in a white girl. I say that makes sense, racial relations be damned. And I say Diedra had something else she gave…No kind of shy or coy or afraid. Shit, she had *me* afraid, thinking she was going to bust me into tiny fragments of bone.

We were out at Font's Point in the Trans Am. This must have been four or five in the morning, after our night shift. That engine was still ticking when she grabbed my hand and shoved it between her legs, started grinding into me like I was dried peppers. I found my way into her seat and we somehow disentangled our clothes bit by bit. I about put my head into her mouth—I might as well have been mining for silver. You know this kind of loving: It's all sweaty and wet, a kind of ceremony all shot through with grunts. She got me into the passenger seat—a new boy called Hardy singing on the country station—and it went just like that, all grunts and sweat, nails scratching through skin, a shattering yelp from her when both of us went.

Well, shit. Me and the wife hadn't made it in a few months and I didn't know what to say.

Diedra said, "You fuck like you been in jail."

"I have," I said. "In a way."

"You ever had a black girl?" She batted her eyes at me and bit the tip of my nose.

"Ah, damn!"

She grinned at me. "Have you?"

"I'll tell you…How I was brought up…I mean, shit—"

"You never fucked a black girl before," she said. "How'd you like it?"

"It has its advantages." She put her head on my chest and we lay there, naked and breathing into each other, a black flower folded into a white one, two kinds of ink swirled together.

Me and Diedra fucked for months. We fucked so much my dick got raw and red, swelled up like a hot dog on the grill. Me and her thought we were smart. Only thing we were was smart for each other. It wasn't long before the rumors started. And the rumors that got the most power are the ones that happen to be true. One thing Diedra never told me: She had a man at home. He was big and black and he sure as shit did not want a white boy fucking his wife.

Look at me, thinking I had it all figured. Shit, for a minute or two, I thought I might have been Dr. Martin Luther King reincarnated. I guess that's the racist in me, thinking a few good fucks can erase the plight of black America.

Like I said, I was brought up a dirty white boy, and I don't know no different.

5

It don't take a college boy to tell you: Me and Diedra getting it on got out on the town, one way or another. The first son of a bitch to call me on it was Preacher Davis. I'm walking out of church after Sunday service, I got the wife on my arm and the kids bringing up the rear, and he pulls me aside like he wants a wet kiss behind the ear. We got wedged in the shadows of a doorway and he said, "You don't think your old lady will know? You don't think God will have you answer Him?" I scratched my nose and scowled.

"Answer Him for what?"

"Don't play dumb with me. That black girl is what. *Her*."

"Her?"

"Yes. *Her*. She's a dirty trick, and she's playing it on you— the girl is devil's music." Preacher Davis had lips so wet they'd never been dry and a nose that ran like a small town beer tap. He wiped it with the back of a hand.

"Devil's music, huh?" I chuckled. My dick got hard thinking about Diedra, that wet warm place down there between her legs. I wished I could stab the preacher to death with the sharp edge of my cock—motherfucker. "I guess you trying to say she's rock 'n' roll, huh? You trying to say she's the reincarnation of Elvis?"

He sneered. "Elvis wouldn't come back a girl. Besides, we don't believe in reincarnation around here you son of a…"

"Son of a what?"

He looked at me with that stupid freaky sneer and wandered off, started giving shoulder rubs to a grandma spinning in a wheelchair. I always hated church and never did find a religious leader who wasn't a conman or pederast. You probably know all about that.

Of course, it didn't take long after that for the wife to get ahold of this information. I knew it was over between us, or just getting started, when she broke a casserole dish over my head while I was watching the Dallas Cowboys piss the bed against the Saints that very evening. Crash! That's all I heard and felt—no pain or nothing. I woke up with blood in my eyes and the wife straddling me, that cold slab of meat plowing into me—this bitch knocked me out with a casserole dish and raped me while I was unconscious. I come to and she's pinching her own nipples, eyes closed in a sick kind of pleasure. Reminded me of one of those Gila monsters they got over in Arizona. She let it go and I did too—sometimes you can't help it—and next thing I know she was standing over me with a pair of garden shears. Believe me, I shook that concussion faster than a Big Ten quarterback. I popped up, wiping blood from my eyes and said, "You are one crazy bitch."

"I might be crazy, but I'm married to you," she said. "Seen and blessed by God His Savior. And there ain't a goddamn thing you can do about it." She snipped the shears a couple times and grinned at me. "You dip that thing of yours in black ink and I swear to fuck I'll chop it off, take you down to a thumb."

I gulped and said, "I don't know what in the hell you're talking about."

"Sure you don't," she said. "Sure you don't."

Those shears snip-snipped in the air and I thought: Good God Almighty—I'm gonna have to murder my way out of this shindig. I got to kill my way out of this.

6

Me and Diedra kept up with the fucking. As hard as we could. And dirty, too. We fucked on the night shift, wherever there wasn't a security camera, and on the back loading dock. Both of us bent into it like stray dogs, Diedra grabbing me by the hair and pulling. She left red scratch marks all over me and I had to tend to myself with ice cubes from the break room. Best about all of it was we had the rhythm between us—I'm talking about the rhythm. Both of us at once, together, all the time. You know what I'm saying. One time, we fucked in the parking lot, two lovebirds grinding it out against the cold pavement. Everybody knew it, too. From Rick Eber on down to the armored car guys who came on Tuesday evenings. Some rumors, they get out there, and you do all you can to make them real. Like trying to keep up with your own shadow. Me and Diedra were doing some of that—keeping up with our shadows. I couldn't stay away from her. She was all I thought about.

Same time, things got more confusing with the wife. First, she stopped waking up before me, putting the coffee on the burner. She slept until ten or eleven, snoring in bed like a fucking elephant. I noticed she got her hair done, too. Blonde highlights that cost me more than a Die-Hard truck battery. I am telling you: All this confused me.

I started sniffing around and saw she had a coupon for a tanning joint downtown, another one for a Brazilian wax place. I started thinking she was planning to corner me, maybe knock my ass out again and fuck me for the horror of it. For about a week, I tried to avoid her—went to work early and came home after she was asleep, my skin and dick still burning from being with Diedra.

It was an uneasy time.

Funny to say, but Diedra turned me on to the truth. We were sticky in the driver's seat of the Trans Am, Diedra perched on me like a bird. Willie Nelson playing a nice solo on Trigger and she said to me, "She got a wax, you said?"

"Yeah—surprised the hell out of me. I ain't been close enough to grin at it, but she got it all mowed."

"And highlights?"

"Cost me a day's fucking pay."

Diedra toppled off me into the passenger seat, started picking at a toenail. "You ever see her working out?"

I thought about it and, damn, Diedra was right. "I think it

was last Monday, she said something about a class." I snapped my fingers trying to think of the name. "It's a word—looks like pirate."

"Pilates?"

"Goddamn. That's it. Down at the YMCA, I think."

Diedra stopped picking at her toe and stretched those muscular legs—like a gymnast, those legs—across the dashboard. I said, "You give me ten minutes, and I'm about to go again."

"I'm always ready for round two," she said. "You might want to head home though—your old lady is fucking somebody."

"Yeah, you're right," I said, not thinking. "My old lady is fucking some—" And it struck me like lightning. My old lady was fucking somebody. Somebody who wasn't me. And this is what's odd about it: I had a beautiful woman in the seat beside me, a woman who I just made yelp like a coyote, and she wanted me again, but…I imagined my wife with another man and—well, Jesus-shit—I wanted to crush somebody. My cheeks got hot and I felt blood in my forehead. Even my hard-on got harder. Don't let me tell you this anger was about anything but power. That's all it was about. I thought, how dare that bitch step out on me? Diedra knew it got to me and she said, "Let me drive you back to the truck."

That's the only thing that stopped the two of us from fucking. We were peace on Earth, her black and me white, but we ended it all by the light of rage—the way most good things end.

7

We were teenagers, we used to call it the beast with two backs—all that fire and brimstone language coming out of us. And that's what this was: A dark room and noises coming from inside it. I heard grunts and thumps, a series of yes's and no's and okay's. I heard that grating voice on the wife, saw her big chicken-eating mouth in my head. And I saw the shadow on the wall, the beast with two backs. Making sounds and smells and odd squeaks that made me cringe. My wife, *the wife*, fucking some guy in our bed.

I reached for the wall and flipped the light switch. The whole scene came into view:

He was big as hell, scary-big even to me, back and shoulder muscles bulging like elephant veins. And she was down under him, grinding up at his midsection like a fiend. It was hellish what I saw, all that sweat and sex liquid pouring off them. He turned to look at me, glassy-eyed and high, but didn't stop. She saw me too, but there was nothing that could distract them. I told you this was a love at first sight story? It wasn't me and Diedra who had it…It was the wife and her new man. They saw me and they kept at it.

Like I didn't exist.

And that's what set me off, what put me into the frame of mind to do what I did.

I had to bring myself back to life, back into existence.

I used the pump-action in the closet. A shell for each of them, and served while they ground each other into oblivion, still fucking while I poured them from this life into the next. Blood and brains and bone. The smell of sex and gunfire. My heart beating endless over theirs.

Some things—even death—can't hold a skinny pole to love.

*

8

Diedra's last letter:

White Boy,

I miss you. That's for damn sure. I miss fucking you, that shiny thing poking into me. I miss that sweat on your chin. Your tongue. I never saw it coming. Roddie stepping out on me. Least of all with some white bitch. That offend you? I doubt it. I bet you never saw a big black guy put it to your wife, huh? Roddie ate too much of that protein powder. Worked his ass out twice a day. Those muscles never got me going. Not like you. Damn. I guess you got another 19 years in the joint. I don't know what it's like in there. I just hope some big bastard doesn't make you his bitch. You don't deserve that. You don't deserve any of this. I guess it's the power of love that got to all of us. We did the whole thing wrong. I miss you. My white boy. I miss you.

Loving,

Your Black Rose

I fold all her letters into squares, hide them in a slit in my mattress. I wish to God Himself she'd send me a goddamn nudie picture. I wish to hell she'd bottle some of her juices and smuggle them into the joint, let me shoot it all up straight into the veins of my… Well, you get the image. You get it. I told you how, where I'm from, mama tells you not to touch that black ink? Now, I know why. Once you had it… There's nothing else for you. Nothing else in the world.

People hear my story, they're gonna call me a racist. What can I say? I was born like this. Or someone made me like this. Or a little bit of both. I know I loved a black girl. And she loved me back. But I also know this: In the joint, it's the white boys gonna keep me breathing. I see it now, a big black guy called Demon eye-fucking me across the commissary. He's waiting for the right time. Or maybe he's waiting for the wrong time. All he wants is a good time.

Kind of funny that way, racial relations.

"You aren't cut out for this, Terry. Pardo isn't either. Problem is, he don't know it."

Trevor Holliday

Don't You Think This Outlaw Bit's Done Got Out of Hand?

The way Terry Matador looked at it, he wasn't involved in the job. Pardo insisted he was. Pardo said Terry was at least an accessory after the fact, and maybe before the fact, too. Anyway, who was going to believe the getaway driver's say-so?

Pardo spent a full day talking Terry into taking the Roadrunner to Laughlin, then California. They needed to get out of town, Pardo said. Misty listened to Pardo, not saying much. Nobody knew where Terry and Pardo were going except maybe Misty.

The big cowboy waved his hand against the uninterrupted blue sky over the river.

Welcome to Laughlin.

An FM radio was playing Peter Frampton where he did that thing with the guitar.

The man in the green short-sleeved poly western shirt rang the little bell on the front desk.

Do you feel like we do?...

The woman came out from the back and gave the man the once-over. She didn't notice he was favoring his right side and of course she couldn't see the bandage on his leg.

The woman turned down the radio. The man asked her about his friends who came in last night driving the purple Plymouth Roadrunner. They both could see the car through the motel office window. No, he didn't want her to call up there to the room. No need to call. He would let them sleep in. They probably were pretty beat. The woman stubbed her cigarette into a plaid beanbag ashtray. She said they were in 227 and pointed to the second floor of the motel.

The man peeked on the registration card. Fake names and the license number was wrong. They did that much right.

No, he wasn't going to need his own room, he was just here for the day.

"Gonna be hot," she said. She was maybe thirty. The man couldn't say.

"Sure is," he said. "A scorcher."

She rolled her eyes. A *you're-not-kidding* look.

"I guess I'll get some breakfast," the man said. "You got any place you recommend?"

"One place here's same as the other," she said. "There's a Denny's down the block."

Upstairs from the office inside 227, the room was black.

Waking from fitful sleep, Terry Matador heard the knock on the door. He tugged the brown vertical blind just enough to let the morning sun into the dark motel room for a couple seconds. He slept in his jeans and T-shirt, the same clothes he wore for the last two days.

Terry was in trouble. Baylor might be dead, but that was

just the start of Terry's problems. Terry would never have been in this situation if Red Pardo minded his own business, but you might as well ask a leopard to change its spots.

Terry was angry at himself. He should have gotten a wake-up call. He should have left hours earlier. But he'd been tired, and he figured Pardo would stay in the casino so long he wouldn't wake up until the early afternoon. He couldn't see who was outside the door. Housekeeping wouldn't be coming to this room until after he left.

Terry figured Pardo would be in the casino by now.

There was another knock on the door.

This was a cheap motel. A beige room with a hollow door. Terry Matador knew something about construction. This motel was made from chicken wire and stucco. You could put your fist through this wall if you wanted. Terry and Pardo put carpet into a hundred rooms built just as flimsy as this one. Places along Ajo Way and Benson Highway in Tucson where rooms were rented by the week.

This door wouldn't hold up to a good shaking let alone somebody putting their boot through it.

Somebody was still standing outside the door. Still knocking.

Maybe Pardo forgot his key. Who else would it be?

"Open the door, Terry."

It wasn't Pardo.

The voice belonged to Baylor. Lower than his normal tone. Baylor's voice sounded strained but under control.

So, Baylor wasn't dead. He got shot outside the trailer, but he wasn't dead.

Terry grabbed the Raven .25 he slipped under his pillow last night. He should have gotten one of the bigger guns the man offered. The others were cannons compared to the Raven. Terry rolled off the side of the bed farthest from the door, head barely clearing the sharp corner of the bedside table. He made a noise falling off the bed.

Baylor didn't react. He didn't smash through the door.

"Lemme in, Terry," Baylor said. "I'm not looking for you. I'm looking for Pardo."

Terry left Red Pardo in the casino last night, rocking one of the video poker machines. Holding a cup of quarters in one hand, a cup for his Copenhagen in the other. Cowboy shirt sleeves rolled up to show the *Rat Fink* tattoo. Singing a little bit to himself over the addictive sounds of the casino hum about knowing when to hold 'em.

That was Red Pardo. A regular Kenny Rogers.

Pardo said poker machines took more skill than the regular one-armed bandit machines, but he never showed Terry evidence to back his claim.

"We gotta talk," Baylor said. "You need to open the door, Terry."

Now, Terry knew what he should have done back at the trailer.

At the trailer there hadn't been time to think.

He should have gunned the car. He should have peeled out of the parking lot just as soon as Baylor got shot. He should have left Pardo there.

Pardo might have gotten shot too, but that wouldn't have been any of Terry's concern.

"We got nothing to talk about, Baylor," Terry said. "This is the end of the line as far as I'm concerned."

"You need to think a little more carefully, Terry," Baylor said. "You got a couple things to consider before you make up your mind."

Terry liked hanging out with Pardo at first.

They worked together, so it seemed natural to go have some beers together after work and sometimes on the weekend. Terry helped Pardo and his girlfriend move their furniture and their mattress from Flowing Wells into their new place near Catalina. Terry mostly did it to help Misty, Pardo's girlfriend. He felt sorry for Misty, the way Pardo treated her.

Holding the Raven, Terry low-crawled from the bed to a spot behind the desk where the television sat. Pulled his knees up and bent his head down. He could have been waiting for a nuclear blast. The desk was substantial enough for Terry to hide behind, at least for the moment. If Pardo came in quickly, Terry would see him first. The desk would be between the two men.

Baylor would be carrying a real gun. Probably the one Pardo said he took to the trailer. Even if Baylor missed, the desk in front of Terry would explode in a cloud of particle board and glue. Terry wouldn't stand a chance against Baylor.

Terry looked at the Raven. The thing was smaller than the palm of his hand.

Maybe the gun was accurate, probably it was not.

It was better than nothing but not much.

Before the mess happened at the trailer, Terry bought the Raven .25 on 22nd Street from a place selling surplus. Pardo got Terry to give him a ride to the place. He told Terry both of them needed guns. Pardo was shocked Terry didn't own one.

Pardo bought a .44 Smith and Wesson Special.

Terry Matador's neighbor back in Tucson was named Lester Manning. Lester lived across the alley from the place Terry used to live. Lester drove an International Scout. Both Lester and the International Scout were built like fireplugs.

There was a bumper sticker on the Scout:

When Guns are Outlawed Only Outlaws Will Have Guns.

A lot of words for one decal.

Terry Matador talked to Lester a couple times out in his back yard. Listening to the cicadas, which nested in the mesquite tree. Terry and Lester smoked cigarettes, drank coffee. Lester Manning served in the Pacific after Pearl Harbor. You couldn't decipher his sailor tattoos anymore. Lester didn't want to talk about the action he'd seen, but Terry imagined he'd seen plenty. Lester Manning said he was going to teach Terry Matador how to play chess, but he hadn't gotten around to it yet.

Terry respected the old guy. Lester Manning didn't mess around. He still looked like he could whip your ass.

Terry wished he was back in Tucson in his place off North First Avenue instead of here in Laughlin. Chances were good Lester Manning would never teach him chess.

He made the mistake of telling Pardo about the chess.

Pardo laughed.

"Hell," Pardo said. "All you gotta do is go to jail. Better yet, get yourself a prison stretch. You can learn the hell out of chess there, son."

Terry Matador didn't like the way things were turning out.

He was hiding behind a wood desk in a chicken wire motel, holding a .25 automatic that looked like a paperweight. He felt like he was gonna puke.

Terry didn't even know if the gun would shoot straight.

He didn't know what Baylor was going to do out there next to the door.

The guy at the surplus store on 22nd Street kept a straight face selling the piece to Terry, even after he'd sold the Smith to Pardo.

"That's not a bad firearm," the man said. "You can do a lot worse for the money, and at least it's made in the USA."

The guy threw in a box of ammunition, too, like Terry was going on a hunting expedition with this little gun.

Baylor would be holding more than a .25 caliber in his hand.

Enough of the blinds were open for Terry to get a look at the twenty-foot cowboy towering over the parking lot at the casino down the street.

Welcome to Laughlin.

Day or night, you could see the big old electric cowboy waving over the river, long before you arrived.

Pardo wasn't playing the machines in the big cowboy casino. Pardo liked playing farther down the strip.

Pardo and his theories.

"I don't wanna pay for the electric bill these places got," Pardo said. "The money they put through these signs? That's loser's money, Bubba."

That was why Pardo liked Laughlin better than Vegas. Not as much overhead he said.

Terry would not listen to Pardo again. Even if Pardo cajoled, offered him more money. Even if Pardo said he would shine Terry Matador's boots every week for a whole damn year.

Nothing was worth working with Pardo again.

And now it turned out Baylor wasn't dead.

Terry Matador and Red Pardo knew how to cut rug and lay it down on smooth concrete. That's maybe all they really knew how to do. They did it all week long back in Tucson for a guy called himself the Carpet King. Talk about original, right? The Carpet King being an Arab guy, he shoulda called himself the Carpet Sheik. The Carpet King was baldheaded and suntanned and had a nice-looking old lady. Terry remembered *her*. The Carpet King's old lady was young, but not that young. She was nice and tan and wore things showed off a good figure. One time Terry saw her wearing some kind of velour cover over a green bikini and she smiled at Terry.

Her name was Nikki. Terry knew that much about her.

He probably wouldn't see Nikki again, either.

The Carpet King looked like Telly Savalas. He always wore a nice poly shirt, chains around his neck, smoked a Tiparillo. Terry Matador drove the van carrying the crew which, until Baylor showed up, was just Terry and Pardo.

Terry got along pretty good with the Carpet King. Terry was the only one of the three who talked to the guy. Why not? The Carpet King liked to kid around, calling the crew *Terry and the Pirates*. Terry even got him to do the Kojak thing a couple times.

Who loves ya, baby?

You could tell the Carpet King was used to the routine because he did it pretty good. Terry figured he himself was on his way up in the business.

Maybe someday he could be the Carpet Prince. Not now though.

This was what happened:

The porta-john the three of them used on their last carpet job backed up to a temporary trailer.

This job was out in the middle of nowhere.

Pardo went back of the building they were working on to use the porta-john. Taking his time about it too, leaving Terry to do the last of the finish.

Terry was making sure the rug was just right, working his way around with the carpet kicker. His knees killing him like they always did. He wondered where Pardo was but figured Pardo was smoking a doobie at the end of the job. Leaving the last part for Terry.

Pardo heard the men inside the trailer and then really started to listen.

If they had seen Pardo, they would have shot him. No question about it. These men were part of a ring. They specialized in gold and silver. The cash was from the jobs they worked. They weren't just working Tucson either. This was a big operation. Mesa, Chandler, Scottsdale. Pardo heard them talking about the money they were bringing in. Pardo saw some of it on the utility table. But this was just the start. They were talking about what was going to happen next Tuesday.

The men didn't know Pardo was in the porta-john or they wouldn't have been talking so loud. Pardo got out of the porta-john and climbed up the chain link fence in back of the temporary trailer. He worked his way through some thorny bougainvillea first, then he slid a milk crate under the window, the crazy bastard. Lucky for him the men hadn't seen him looking in. There were three men in the trailer. The place was paneled like somebody's living room with a water cooler, some file cabinets, and folding chairs. Coffeemaker on the table, but the men were drinking San Miguel beers. The men wore guns on their sides. They meant business. There were a couple telephones on the utility tables in the place and one of the men was on the phone the whole time Pardo was peeking in the window.

"Man, I saw guns and a whole lotta cash," Pardo said. "Stacks of cash these dudes had."

"They didn't see you?" Terry Matador said.

"Unh-uh," Pardo said. He shook his head. "Dudes might not even known there was a window there."

"You're lucky they didn't," Terry said.

"I'm going back," Pardo said. "Something's gonna happen Tuesday."

Terry didn't think much about the story, except for wondering why Pardo didn't just mind his own business.

Pardo didn't tell Terry what he was planning.

Terry didn't think much about Pardo's story. So there were men in the trailer with cash. So what? Pardo was always talking. Then Tuesday, Pardo got Terry to drive around front of the trailer while he and Baylor got out and walked up to the place.

Two days ago.

It felt like a month since then.

"Just wait a minute here, Terry," Pardo said.

Terry drove the Roadrunner to the front of the trailer. Pardo and Baylor got out of the car.

"We're just going in here for a minute. Baylor wants to take a look at these dudes."

Terry heard Baylor when the two were walking away from the car.

"That's all you told him?" Baylor said. "Are you putting me on? You didn't tell him?"

Like a dope, Terry Matador waited for Pardo and Baylor outside the trailer.

He kept the Roadrunner going with his foot on the accelerator.

"Don't turn the car off, Terry," Pardo said. "We might gotta fly out of here."

Terry should have figured what Pardo was up to, but he hadn't. Everything happened quickly.

Baylor and Pardo walked into the trailer cool as could be, those two.

Terry didn't see the guns they were carrying. Didn't see them put masks on. According to Pardo, neither did the dudes in the trailer.

Pardo said they threw down on the men so fast the men didn't know what was going on.

"You put on masks?" Terry said.

"What do you think," Pardo said. "You think we're dumb?"

That was when Terry started thinking about the purple Roadrunner. The car was close to twelve years old and there weren't a whole lot of them on the road. Anybody started looking, they could find that car.

Pardo didn't want to talk about Terry's car. He wanted to talk about Baylor.

Pardo said Baylor screwed up. One guy came out of the back while Pardo stuffed cash in a bag.

The guy shot Baylor.

Pardo left him.

Got into the Roadrunner by himself.

"Get going, Terry," he said.

Terry didn't know what was going on, but he heard shots, so he hit the gas.

Pardo said Terry was into the thing up to his neck as an accessory, on account of he was driving the car and took money from Pardo.

"Think the cops are gonna believe you didn't know what was going down?" Pardo said. "Baylor's back there dead. He took his eye off the ball. Those dudes in the trailer are gonna come after us, so it's not the cops you gotta think about."

Not that it made any difference now, but if he knew what was going on, Terry would have turned Pardo down flat.

Pardo walked away with twenty-seven hundred and forty-eight dollars because that was what was on the table. Pardo gave Terry four bills for driving. Counted the bills out like he was a big man.

Maybe he would have split the bread with Baylor, he didn't say.

"Too bad about Baylor," Pardo said. That was it.

Terry Matador drove away, still not knowing what happened.

"I don't know," Pardo said. "There weren't any coins on the table. Least I didn't see any. You think I shoulda made them empty their pockets?"

Pardo told Terry the whole story about Baylor when Pardo and Terry were driving away.

Pardo wouldn't have done the job without Baylor. Baylor gave Pardo the idea he was some kind of pro. Baylor started talking to Pardo after work a few weeks ago right when he started working for the Carpet King. The man wasn't any good with carpets, but he could talk. Drinking beers on Grant Road, Baylor started dropping hints to Pardo about his shoot 'em up skills and his outlaw past.

It didn't take much to impress Red Pardo.

Baylor knew the layout of a bank near Davis-Monthan which would be simple to knock over. Was this something Pardo would be interested in? Baylor didn't want to know right then. Just think about it.

The bank was always heavy with cash right after payday at DM when the flyboys cashed their paychecks. There was a bar next to the place Baylor said he could take Pardo if he wanted. Baylor knew all about the bank because he dated a teller worked at the place. Well, she *was* a teller there, but she'd left for personal reasons. Now she was working at a bar on Speedway and Baylor didn't go there much, so things were like that.

One thing Baylor told Pardo, he knew how to scout a location.

"That's what he told me, Terry," Pardo said. "He said he would always scout a place, but if it didn't look right, he wouldn't do the job."

"You're telling me this now?" Terry said. "You shoulda told me what you were doing."

Pardo just shook his head and said just listen.

Baylor told Pardo he put on a good Ban-Lon shirt and some slacks and gone up and talked to the assistant manager of the bank about starting an account for his mother. Baylor got a short haircut and combed it with Brylcreem. The bank manager just figured Baylor was stationed at DM. Baylor asked how much cash he needed to put in, how easy it would be to make withdrawals, whether she would get a complimentary savings deposit box for her valuables and so on. All at the same time, Baylor's making a mental map of the place, checking out the locations of the video cameras, assessing the mobility of the man working security at the front door.

Baylor thanked the assistant manager, a man named Jerry Furness. Asked Furness if he needed to bring his mother in to start the account. Baylor said his mother had her good days and her bad days. Furness shook his head no. Just come in when you're ready. He stood up and shook Baylor's hand.

Baylor figured the place was perfect.

Except it wasn't. He announced this to Pardo the next day. No, he didn't want to go into details, but forget it, it won't work. Place was filled with undercover men. His girlfriend didn't think to tell him this at first, but thankfully he'd called her one more time just to go over things.

They didn't just leave security to the one guy by the door. Are you kidding? She said security was undercover. In and out through the day. Even the tellers at the bank didn't know who was packing a gun. Maybe Jerry Furness himself.

Baylor said he'd been pissed at first his ex-girlfriend didn't tell him this but then he'd gotten over it, life being too short. At least she told him.

Pardo was relieved. He figured they were getting a little too close to a trip to the Florence prison for his tastes. Bank robbery is chancy at best, and Pardo didn't want to get locked up. He'd been thinking about a way to get out of this thing with Baylor anyway.

Then Pardo and Baylor drank some more. Pardo told Baylor what he'd seen in the window of the temporary trailer. He heard the men talking about more money coming on Tuesday. Robbing thieves made more sense to Pardo than robbing a bank.

Baylor wanted to know more. He said he would check the trailer out.

Terry Matador didn't know what to do. Baylor wasn't going to just stand there outside the door.

"Open up, Terry," Baylor said. "I'm not fooling around. Open up or I'm coming in."

Terry Matador looked at the Raven. Closed his eyes. Tried to think.

The phone rang.

"Answer it," Baylor said. "If that's Pardo, tell him I'm here.

The phone was on the desk. Terry reached up and answered it.

It was Pardo. Terry didn't ask him where he was.

"Baylor's here," Terry said.

Loud enough so Baylor can hear.

"He's outside the room. He says he needs to see you."

"Ask him what he wants," Pardo said.

"I'm not asking him that," Terry said. "You know what he wants. He's outside this room."

"Tell him to wait," Pardo said. "Five minutes. Ten maximum. I'll be there."

Terry hung up the phone.

"He says he'll be here in a few minutes," Terry said. "He says just wait."

"I'll give him five minutes," Baylor said, "I'm serious, Terry. I don't mean you any harm. Pardo was the one got me shot. You might as well listen to what I got to tell you."

Terry Matador got out from behind the desk and opened the door. Terry couldn't see Baylor's features because of the contrast of the dark room and the sun's glare.

"You got any coffee made yet?" Baylor said.

He sat in the chair in front of the desk.

Terry shook his head. There was no coffee maker in this room.

"How did you know to come here?" he said.

"Misty," Baylor said. "Pardo is easy to track."

Baylor looked at Terry.

"I'm gonna level with you," he said.

Baylor nodded at the boots Terry took off last night.

"Put those things on, Terry," he said. "You need to get out of here."

"What are you planning to do?" Terry said.

"You don't need to ask that, do you?" Baylor said.

Baylor limped a little sitting down. Held his hand where he'd been shot.

"This still hurts like hell," Baylor said. "I know a woman used to work emergency at Saint Rita's. She took care of it, but I can only stand so much of this."

Baylor pulled his gun out. Put it on his lap. Not holding it exactly, but it was there.

"You aren't cut out for this, Terry," Baylor said.

Terry shook his head. He knew he wasn't.

"Pardo isn't either," Baylor said. "Problem is, he don't know it."

Terry nodded.

"You can still get out," Baylor said. "Don't concern yourself with Pardo."

He got up and pulled the blinds a foot to his right. Looked down.

"He's not coming up yet," Baylor said. "I don't see him. Don't worry. Nothing's gonna happen in this room. Nothing ties you to this. Just that car of yours. I'd do something about it, I were you."

"You don't see him yet?" Terry said.

"I'll give him a couple minutes," Baylor said. "If he's not here by then I'll go find him."

Terry looked at Baylor. The man nodded toward the door.

"I like my Roadrunner," Terry said. "I saved up for it."

Baylor nodded.

"It's a nice one," he said. "But I'm guessing you also like living."

Terry opened the door and looked out over the clear desert sky. He walked down the concrete stairs.

There was nobody in the parking lot. Terry got into the Roadrunner.

No sign of Pardo yet, but Terry knew him.

Pardo would come.

*As each crime progressed,
so did Jesse's need to be somebody more.*

IAN KLINK

I AIN'T LIVING LONG LIKE THIS

Jesse woke up in the dirty motel room with scratches on his back and his pants balled up in the cobwebbed corner. He knew he needed a cigarette, and badly. Setting his bare feet on a carpet stained with what only the Lord was privy to, Jesse walked a few steps before she rolled over to call after him. "Where you going?" she asked.

Jesse turned his head. "That's my business."

Her plump, worn body moved under the sheets and disgusted him a little. "Well, my business is fifty bucks." Jesse smiled at her and walked naked over to the corner to get his pants. His billfold was still in the back pocket, chained to his jeans. He was quite surprised it was still there, considering the company he was with. He grabbed a Jackson, two Hamiltons, and a wad of disarrayed Washingtons and threw them across the bed.

"Asshole," she softly muttered and pulled the grubby bills underneath the soiled sheets. Jesse heard what she called him and fancied the title of honor. He always had. She stuffed the money in a safe spot and asked him if he had a cigarette. Jesse smiled and pulled up his wranglers. He shifted through the pockets of his jacket until he found the pack and hurled it onto the bed. She pulled the lighter from the pack, lit the stick, and the smoke danced toward the ceiling like a sooted ballerina. He could taste its welcoming and grabbed one of his own. She held out the lighter and soon there was a ballroom dance of used smoke twirling around the off-kilter ceiling fan. Jesse winked at her before walking into the bathroom, slamming the door behind him.

It was going to be a sultry day from the heat seeping in the opened window above the broken tiled shower. For ten dollars and some change, it was not the worst motel he ever stayed in. He set his stick down and ran a nice Amish bath. He washed his pits and splashed some water on his need-to-be-shaved face. It had been a long time on the road and, although he thought about getting a razor and some cream, he let it slip by. He thought of the woman in the other room and turned the water hotter. He didn't mind an itch, but never hurt to burn off a skanks presence when warranted.

Splashing some water across his face and running it in his hair, Jesse looked at himself in the mirror. He saw someone he might have once known, but they were long gone. In its place was a legend. A God of the highway whom they would be talking about for years to come. A smile crept from the corners of his ravenous mouth and he needed to attend to some business.

He opened the door as she was pulling on her bra with more ease than he had to get it off. She was startled and got off the bed. She looked around the floor and found her underwear and short skirt rumpled under the bed. "It's already baking," she said, pulling her panties over her growling stomach.

Jesse nodded his head.

She pulled her skirt to fit right and sized him up again. "I could go for another round if you want."

"I'm good..."

"I don't have to charge," she softly said, getting on the bed to crawl towards him on her hands and knees. She stopped on the other side, looking up at him. "You've been so nice to me and all."

"I'm good."

"Then I want some food."

Jesse leaned in. "I want you to get your smelly cunt over here." Jesse pulled out his switchblade. The apical steel blade was still covered in worn dried blood. "That's not fucking funny!" she yelled. She bolted off the bed, yanked her purse, and tried to open the door, but something sharp and frigid entered the small of her back. She could feel the blood running down her back in warm streams. She had just a second to register the tingle in her feet before another stinging pain dug into her back. Her breath disappeared. Her last thought of conscience was 'The Motel Killer' she heard about was the man she just got paid to sleep with. As the blade ripped across her throat, the thought faded and so did she.

He leaned against the doorframe of the bathroom, her blood a mask of death upon his face, and could only laugh. It was not seeing her sprawled dead across the floor, but her blood extinguished his cigarette. As he flicked the crimson stick into the sink, Jesse rubbed her blood into his stubble and thought how he must have looked like all the other men's faces she looked up at night after night. He looked around and inhaled the rottenness of the motel room. He went back to clean himself up and stepped over the dead hooker's body before he left the room. The paper the next morning identified her as a mother of two who had turned to the street to make ends meet and often solicited at the local Highway Rose Motel, where she became the latest victim of 'The Motel Killer.' Her name was Sheila Jenson, aged forty-two years.

It took a few jumps, but Natalie, his trusted fifty-eight Panther 75 Springer, turned and roared like a lion. As he peeled her tires, rocks from the Motel's gravel driveway spurt behind, and a trail of dust rose to the VACANCY sign of the motel. It did not dawn on him until miles down the road he never got her first name.

The trail of weeds, rocks, and faded paint rolled past Natalie's tires as Jesse wandered down the highways of America. He had been running ever since he killed a homeless man named Willy McCoalldry. In the grand scheme of life, Jesse wished there had been a better reason other than Willy trying to grab the chain of his wallet, but not everybody's end can be like Odysseus. Some are born to be the hero and some end up meat for the beast. He always liked that story from what little days of school he attended and often thought of the story while driving down the road, stealing gas from station to station. Jesse would never know the truth—Willy tripped and was only reaching to break his fall, but Willy grabbed the chain of a man with a switchblade and an itchy finger. After Jesse lodged the knife into Willy's throat, feeling the spray of his vivid wet blood fall onto his hands, he jumped onto Natalie and never looked back. Being on parole after serving four years for busting a Five and Dime, he knew he would be sent up forever if caught again, especially for murder. Since then, Jesse had committed more crimes than he cared to think about, from robbing motorists to killing a gas clerk in New Jersey whose only crime was working the night Jesse and Natalie rolled into town. Jesse was confident the clerk recognized his face and stabbed the man twenty-three times before stealing the gas and the cash from his register.

As each crime progressed, so did Jesse's need to be somebody more. A few years back he read of a man who, along with his psychotic girlfriend, had stormed the state of Texas, making bullets rain from their toxic love cloud. Jesse thought *maybe, just maybe, I could be like that*. It was not until Jesse stabbed a door-to-door insurance salesman he knew what his legacy would become. When the salesman left his room open to get some ice, Jesse slid in and stabbed the guy as soon as he walked in, dropping the bucket of ice onto the floor. Looking at one of his cards, Jesse saw his name was Alvin Harsowitz from Long Dale, Pennsylvania. After he stabbed him in the gut several times, he grabbed his cash and gold watch and throttled on down the road. When he checked the morning papers, he was disappointed the killing only made page three. If Jesse DeLoach was going to be a name he had to do better.

The next week he entered the big time: Page one.

Jesse was hanging around a run-down shit-shack named Motel Towers in Shabbona, Illinois, eating a cheeseburger he got at the Tastee Freeze stand, waiting for the right person to make him a star. His wishes came in Doris Tannerman, a retired secretary who took a vacation for the second time in her dull content life. She was going to visit her sister in Denver from what Jesse could gather as she begged for mercy. What Jesse did to her went beyond his mind's comprehension. He should have shown mercy, but getting the name meant more. Hours later he awoke on Natalie, a severed finger wrapped in his jacket, next to a few of her teeth.

When the sheriff entered the motel room, he vomited so much he contaminated the crime scene.

The papers called him 'The Motel Killer' and Jesse was happy.

As he looked down the long road, Jesse was making a name for himself as Natalie was purring. No one was going to stop Jesse DeLoach from taking care of business at every highway motel from here until the front tire dipped into the salty ocean.

After a few more bodies, some news reports, and a couple of states later, Jesse rolled into Digby, Iowa, a town so small a break of wind was a major event. A dilapidated house with men sitting in rocking chairs, a gorgeous brick Methodist church, and the main street post office welcomed Jesse and Natalie with friendly waves from strangers. After seeing an older couple walking hand in hand, Jesse felt like his crime spree would spare this little slice of heaven. He was too hungry and too tired.

He drove up to the only gas station pump in town and shut Natalie off. Gus Simpthorn, who had been working at the station since he was a junior in high school, came up to Jesse, looking over Natalie. "Oh boy," Gus swooned. "Haven't seen a Panther in a few years. How she run?"

"Smooth," Jesse said.

"That's good. Real good," Gus said, looking over Natalie some more. "I guess I can't look under the hood for you?"

Jesse smiled, assuming Gus had used this line a time or two before. "Just fill her."

"Can do," Gus said, pulling off the handle on the pump.

"You got something cold to drink?"

"Hose in the back for water. There's a soda machine around the corner. Twenty-five cents. I know, used to be five," Gus said, shrugging his shoulders.

Jesse dug into his pockets to find a quarter and went around the station.

Pulling a cold bottle of Saratoga Cola out of the machine, Mary Sue thought it was Paul Newman at first when she saw his dirty jeans and dusty jacket.

Jesse thought he saw a teenage devil, wrapped in an angelic body.

Mary Sue could not move, helpless to hide the smile across her freckled face. The heat made the soda sweat and small droplets of mud bubbles formed at her feet. Jesse slowly crept toward her, a wolf edging toward the hens. He started to flip the coin into the air, higher and higher each time, catching it each time with a snap. Mary Sue could feel herself getting wetter with each slide his worn and cracked boots made.

Jesse walked up and leaned against the machine, eyeing her whole body. *If he does not speak, I'm going to die right in front of him* she thought.

"Shame. I would have bought it for you," his smooth voice rolled off his canine fangs, the brightest Mary Sue had ever seen. He flipped the coin in the air again, caught it, and held it out to her. When he opened his hand, the coin was missing.

Mary Sue laughed as only a schoolgirl can. "How?" she found the nerve to ask. Jesse winked at her. "Magic," was all he softly said. He reached behind her hair with the other hand and, like a children's trick, pulled a quarter from behind her ear. Mary Sue's knees locked. She had built a reputation in town for boys, but he was different.

They both thought each was special.

Jesse pulled out a cold bottle, popped the top on the machine, and let the suds burn his throat while cooling the Sahara inside from the ride. He downed the whole bottle in one round and threw the bottle into the overgrown grass field next to the station. He loved hearing the bottle break on some random rock.

Mary Sue held onto the bottle, the wet circle growing at her feet.

"You going to drink that?" he asked.

Mary Sue looked down at her bottle, warm from her hands, and realized she wanted it colder.

As if reading her mind, Jesse grabbed the bottle, caressing her soft hands with his rugged fingers, and placed it on top of the machine. He dug into his pockets for another quarter and pulled out a new cold bottle of Saratoga for her. As he popped the top off, he said "It should be cold, right out of the machine."

"Thank you," she whispered, shyly reaching for it. He pulled it away at the last second and she laughed. He finally let her take it and, to tease him a bit, placed the tip of her tongue in the bottle before lifting it into the air. Mary Sue wanted him.

The image of dragging his blade across her sweat-beaded neck wet his lips again, but Jesse knew she was not worth it. Besides, if it was not in a motel, they might not give him credit for it.

"Hey, mister," Gus called from the corner of the building.

Jesse turned in his direction. "What?"

"You all set to go. Gave it some new oil as well. Needed some."

Jesse paused. No one took care of Natalie but him. "I didn't ask for it."

Gus paused for a second or two, knowing not what to do. The owner usually dealt with strangers, and to protect Gus, but he was out with a nasty summer cold. Gus was all on his own, desperately racking his brain for what to do.

Mary Sue could feel Jesse getting upset and stepped in. "Gus is a little slow," she whispered. "He didn't mean it. I'll pay for it if you need it."

Jesse looked between the two of them before yelling "I'll be there in a second." Gus scratched his head and walked away, fast.

They stood there in silence for a few seconds before Jesse winked at her and started walking around the building.

Mary Sue watched until he turned the corner before placing the bottle on top of the machine and followed after.

As she turned the corner, she saw Gus timidly holding out his hand. Jesse was digging through his pockets for a few bills and slapped them hard into Gus' hand. In his mind, if it had been a different town, Jesse would have taken care of business on Gus, but he had a better reputation now and a legion of followers who expected more. Jesse got on Natalie and she started on the first pump. He looked over at Mary Sue and they locked eyes. She wanted to have him and he wanted to have her. Both for different reasons. Without looking away, he asked Gus "Any place to eat around here?"

"Yup. The diner is up the road about half a mile, next to the Digby Inn." Jesse smiled as he revved the engine. He winked at Mary Sue and left a trail of dust in his wake before getting back on the concrete path to another motel.

He pulled Natalie into the parking lot of the Digby Diner and paused for a second. A few cars down was a Plymouth with some blue squad lights on the top. Suddenly his appetite was not as strong as it had been while on the road.

He knew there was nothing he could do. The cop would no doubt hear Natalie's engine and raise suspicion about a stranger peeling away, so he turned the key, popped the stand, and walked into the diner.

The bell above the door rang as Jesse walked in. The diner was slim for lunchtime. He immediately saw the police officer eating a fried bologna and bacon sandwich. He expected the officer to already be staring at him but the officer was too busy wolfing down the bread with his slightly browned water. Jesse looked over and saw a waitress behind the counter, a cook sweating over the grill, and the elderly couple who held hands in the back booth. Jesse walked forward a few steps, letting the bell ring again as the door shut. Still nothing from anyone.

The waitress stopped wiping the counter and looked at him. "You can sit in any booth. Coffee?"

Jesse shook his head, not wanting the sheriff to hear his voice. They still had no idea what 'The Motel Killer' looked or sounded like, so why start now?

"Alright," she said and started pouring some water for him.

Jesse would have to order something else, knowing to drink the water would be worse than dying. He walked down a bit before sitting in a window booth, always wanting to see who might be on their way to catch him. The browned water was placed in front of him. The waitress pulled out her pad and pencil, but no words. "I'll have a cheeseburger. Rare. Fries as well," he softly spoke.

She wrote it down and walked away, still no words.

Jesse looked out the window and then looked over at the officer, who was finishing his meal. He wiped his mouth and placed his hat back on his head. He reached into his pocket and threw a few bills on the counter. "Great meal, Herb.

Linda," he said walking toward the door. The bell rang and he walked out. Jesse was sure the officer never even saw his face. He looked out the window and the officer avoided Natalie as he got in his squad car. In a few seconds, the car drove down the road, protecting the safe citizens of Digby, Iowa. Jesse laughed at the stupidity. *Could be bumped up to the big time if he only knew how close he was*, Jesse thought. He was so humored by his ego he never noticed he was drinking the pipe-stained water. He was inside his head. He missed the front doorbell ring as she came in. When he set the water down, Mary Sue stood next to his booth. "Can I sit?" she softly asked.

Jesse looked around. The waitress refilled the elders' cups and the cook was still sweating away, droplets falling onto Jesse's food. When he turned back around, he said "Sure." Mary Sue could not get into the booth fast enough. "Thank you, um…" she stopped, realizing she never got his name. She asked for it.

"That's my business," he said.

She paused for a second, thinking of what to say. "Well, mine is Mary Sue."

"Nice to meet you again, Mary Sue. You from here?"

"Lived here all my life."

"Why?"

She shrugged her shoulder. The waitress brought her some water and flipped her book. Before Mary Sue could decline, Jesse leaned forward. "She'll have a cheeseburger as well. Also, a Saratoga, right?" She nodded and the waitress left with nary a word again. "I figured you might want a bite to eat."

"Oh, I do, but I ain't got money."

He smiled. "No worries."

She smiled back and winked at him. He winked back and

her insides warmed. "So, tell me about yourself?" he asked, genuinely curious.

"Not much to tell," she said, and Jesse could hear an itty-bitty pinch of sadness in her voice. "Been here my whole life. Done with it for the most part."

"What do you mean?"

The waitress set his plate down. "Will be a few minutes for hers," she finally spoke.

"Thank you," Mary Sue said as the waitress walked away, silent again.

"Want some?" he asked.

"I'll wait. You're not from around here, are you?"

"That's my business."

"Oh come on. Someone finally comes into this shithole and I want to know why."

Jesse loved her sassiness. "I'm not from around here, no."

"Going anywhere in particular?"

"The ocean."

Mary Sue's eyes bulged. "That's a dream of mine, to see the ocean."

It was Jesse's turn to be curious. "Why?"

"You drove here. Its farms as far as you can see. I'm tired of cow shit and fields of hay. I want to see the ocean, just once."

"Then go."

"Yeah, right."

"Journey of a thousand miles starts with one step," he said, remembering his English teacher's oft-quoted line.

"My papa would kill me… if he would notice."

They always had a story; Jesse felt and knew hers would be just another. Just as sad. Just as dramatic. Just as boring. He took a bite of the cheeseburger and loved it. "This is the best burger I've had since a diner in Ohio."

"Besides," she continued. "I don't have any money, I said."

"You can if you steal it," he said and saw the shock in her eyes. He loved it as much as the burger, biting into another round.

"I want to go to the beach as I hear in…" She stopped and looked over at the Wurlitzer in the corner. She spun around. "Let me borrow a quarter."

He was not sure where this was going, but curiosity killed the cat. He pulled out a few quarters and slid them across to her.

Mary Sue ran over to the Wurlitzer and punched numbers. After a second the hum of the speaker popped and the record dropped. "*Let's all go to a place I want to be. A place where there's just sand and you and me. Let's get to the ocean and put our feet in the sand. We'll drink some fruity punch and listen to the band,*" streamed out of the used speakers. He had heard the song before. She spun around to look at him, dancing like a free bird. "I love this song! Don't you?"

The elderly couple had enough and walked out of the restaurant hastily. Jesse could care less, looking at this angelic devil shaking her body forbiddingly in broad daylight. She slapped her hands together, mouthing the words of the tune across her innocent lips. She closed her eyes and Jesse knew she was seeing the ocean behind her eyes, the waves slapping against the coastal rocks, an image foreign to Digby, Iowa.

Jesse liked her. She was brave. She was cute. She was dangerous.

The cook finally had enough and moved away from the grill. "Knock it off, goddammit! I told you before!"

"Oh, stuff a duck!" Mary Sue shouted back.

"Hey!" the waitress shouted. "You don't talk to us like that, Mary Sue!"

"I'll say whatever I want!"

"You little shit!" The cook muttered under his breath and

started to take off his apron. "I've had enough of you."

Mary Sue opened her eyes and spun around, looking at the sweaty old man charging toward her.

Jesse already had his hand inside his pocket before the cook came around the counter. The cook was about to grab her shoulders when the snap of his steel blade stopped him dead in his tracks. Jesse was out of the booth, waving the switchblade in his hand. "Don't fucking touch her, you fatso!"

The waitress dropped her coffee pot onto the floor and screamed as it splashed on her legs. It was an older pot or it would have melted her skin. She wanted to grab her legs but was afraid to move.

Jesse moved from the waitress's eyes to the cook's, each terrified. He stepped forward and waved his knife for the waitress to come around the counter. She slowly began to shuffle her feet between sniffles. "Move!" Jesses demanded. She timidly screamed and hurried out behind the counter and stood next to the cook. "Mary Sue, come over here," Jesse softly ordered.

Mary Sue looked at him and at a slow pace walked towards him. When she was close enough, Jesse grabbed her behind him. He switched the blade to his other hand and ran over to lock the front door before anyone else showed up at the party. "Get on your knees. Now!" The cook and the waitress obliged. Her eyes were shut so tight you could see her pulse move the thin flesh.

Jesse walked forward and was going to take care of them both when he heard another song drop under the Wurlitzer's needle. *It's that time of the summer, to be cool and drive. Feel the breeze through your hair and be alive.* Jesse remembered her dream. While looking at the two on the floor, he called for her. "Mary Sue, come here."

She took a second and slowly walked up to him. "Yes," a shrill voice uttered.

"You want a free ticket to your dreams?" he asked, waving his knife.

"Yes," she whimpered, not realizing what to do.

"Then come here," he said and spun around to be behind her, holding her in his arms. "Take the knife."

The cook went to move and Jesse moved fast to slam his chipped boot into the cook's sweaty eye socket, shattering the bone and slicing the soft meat of his cornea. He fell backward, holding his eye and screaming in pain. The cook had a tattoo on his forearm he got in the middle of the Pacific Ocean from his buddy Jimmy Carlino. He had thought that was painful. He was wrong. The waitress reached her arms around him, crying herself, and did her best to comfort him.

"You do that again, and I'll slice it out!" Jesse screamed. He went back to placing the knife in Mary Sue's hand and looked her in the eye. "You do it."

"What?"

"Take care of them and you can come with me."

Mary Sue shook her head and dropped the knife on the floor, slowly backing away.

"Stop," he calmly said, and within his calmness she obeyed.

The cook wined some more and Jesse turned to kick him in the stomach. The waitress screamed so loud it hurt Jesse's ears and his fist met her jaw and she fainted on the floor. The cook rushed and slammed into Jesse's stomach. They both crashed into a table and fell onto the floor. As they tussled, age before beauty let Jesse get on top and he slammed his closed fist into the cook's swelled eye. It was too much for the cook and he gave up. Jesse stood and slammed his boots down hard on the cook's bulldog face.

"No!" Mary Sue screamed through her clenched fists.

Her scream made Jesse stop and let the beast calm down for a second.

She was scared.

Jesse thought for a second. He walked over to the door, unlocked it, and motioned for her to head on out.

Mary Sue refused to move, needing to know. "What are you going to do?"

"That's my business."

It took her a while to get to the door, and when she was next to him, she paused. She looked him in the eye. Jesse was not sure what they were saying. Mary Sue shut the door and latched the lock. She looked over toward his blade on the ground. She walked over to pick it up and held it out to Jesse.

He was stunned. He reached out slowly and even pulled back for a moment before getting it from her. He looked into her as best he could.

"I want to watch," she said, the thirst behind every utterance.

Jesse smiled and took care of business.

Twenty-five minutes later, covered in their blood, Jesse unlatched the bolt and headed into the fiery sun. He could whiff the copper stink swathing his clothes. Mary Sue shuffled behind him, her clothes as clean as before.

Jesse hopped onto Natalie and she started on pump three. He knew the oil change was a mistake and wanted to rip the heart out of Gus before he left. He revved the engine a little bit, kicking the stand up, and pulled Natalie out of the parking space. He knew he would have to find a well or something down the road to get the blood off. "I have to go. You coming?" he asked.

She had grown up in the past twenty-five minutes. There was no turning back now. "To California? To the Pacific?"

"Natalie's front tire is going right into the waves."

Mary Sue hopped on the back of Natalie and hugged his waist. Jesse peeled away toward the edge of town. No one seemed to mind their exit. An old man waved at them from the front porch. Mary Sue waved back and hollered, "Goodbye, Mr. Rydell!"

As the road led them out of town, Mary Sue hugged him tighter. Jesse looked over his shoulder and then toward the horizon. The sun was moving across the sky. For miles on end, they never saw so much as a single car. They stopped by an old farm along a country road to wash up. As he rung the blood out of his jacket as best he could, Jesse could see just how much of a grown woman she was close to being.

Mary Sue wanted to be with him forever.

As the sun was setting across the amber horizon, Jesse saw a billboard for 'vacancy' at the Kelchin Motel. He pointed at the sign so Mary Sue could see it.

"Why are we stopping?" she asked.

"That's my business," he answered.

January Bain

Gold Dust Woman

1969 Nashville Saturday Night

She caught Hunter's attention the second she strolled through the concert gate in her red silk blouse and tight blue jeans. A pretty little thing with golden hair down to her ass and a gold dust sprinkling of freckles across her button nose. She owned her shit, smiled like she had the bigger picture in mind when their paths crossed. But our MC club had been hired to provide protection for the musicians, not chase pussy. Besides, the summer of love was long gone and decided in its infinite wisdom to skip him.

He nodded at the vision. She was so above his pay grade he could just be himself, not bother to impress. Yeah, keep telling himself that, it might work. She stared, then pointed at his colors. "Hell's Angels. You ride?"

"Yeah, you looking to ride?" He also owned his shit.

She came closer while her two girlfriends lagged behind, near enough he could see the yellow highlights in her pale blue eyes. Her perfume reminded him of sweet peas on a hot summer's day back home in Montana. Of verandas and porch swings and Sunday fried chicken dinners. Long ways from Oakland where he now found himself.

"I'm thinking of getting my own bike. Saved up plenty, enough to pretty much get any model I want. So yeah, I'm looking to ride."

"Gotta work now, but hang around after the concert and I'll take you for one on my Bad Boy."

Her smile widened. "A Harley. Maybe. We'll see."

"Wasn't talking about my bike. What's your name, Sweet Cheeks?"

She left with a parting shot of her own. "Not Sweet Cheeks. But I'm guessing yours should be Hot Stuff." She linked arms with her two girlfriends and they danced off, taking his interest with them.

He overheard one say, "Are you crazy! Does he know who your father is?"

"And you're not to tell him I'm related to that bastard, you hear me?" Sweet Cheeks said, her voice filled with warning. *Hmm, interesting.*

"Nice piece of ass you were talking up. Prez's asking for you. Got an issue with the venue," Fast Joe said, the chapter's sergeant-in-arms, coming over to join him. His eyes tracked the trio of hot babes walking away.

He couldn't fault Joe for having good taste, smothering a groan. If there was any justice left in the universe, it would be the final countdown to needing to answer the beck and call of the tyrant that called himself Prez of the Oakland chapter.

"I'll check it out," he said. Striding over to the roped-off area in front of the temporary stage, he slipped under the metal chain and over to the visitor's tent where the Prez was huddled with half a dozen other MC members. Everyone was in gang colors, jeans, boots, and cuts for the festival they'd been hired to provide security. How the Prez had managed the feat of getting the gig after the last fiasco he'd never know, except by threat or maybe doing it for free beer again?

"About time, Hunter, this is not the moment to be chasing tail. You can do lots of that later up at Stoner Lodge. Invite her and her friends along. We could use some fresh pussy," Prez said, his mouth twisted in a sneer endearing himself all the more. "We got ourselves a problem. Boyo spotted a member of the Rebel shitheads and they're handing out LSD, peyote, and magic mushrooms like it's goddammed candy, looking to cut in on us, create another turf war. I want payback for what that mealy mouthed singer said about us after Altamont and those assholes are only going to get in the way. Hell, a country and western singer would have handled his shit, not dumped on us like Mr. Can't-get-no-satisfaction did. I want the score settled and that's the end of it."

"Maybe we can use it to our advantage? Lay all the blame on them," he ventured.

Prez narrowed his eyes to slits, lowered his voice to a husky whisper. "You got that gun hidden where I told you, ready for Snake?"

Snake had pulled the short straw at the previous night's church meeting. All church meetings were held at the clubhouse behind closed doors, no exceptions. "Yeah. Behind the toilet tank. Where is Snake?"

"Don't worry about him. Just be ready when I say the word."

"Yeah. Want me to keep an eye on the Rebels? Make it awkward to do business?"

"I don't need you to tell me what needs doing." Prez glared at him.

Appear weak when you are strong, and strong when you are weak. Sun Tzu's quote from the Art of War flitted through his brain. While it kept him on his toes, he itched to strike the man to the ground, then dance on his grave. Talk about no satisfaction.

Snake showed up at that moment, his face pale beneath the long greasy hair, dark beard, and tan.

"Where ya been?" Prez demanded.

The greasy man swiped at his mouth. "That damn burrito I had for breakfast ain't sitting right, pouring out of both ends. Not sure I can handle my shit tonight."

Prez glared at him, making Snake turn even paler and shrink a size or two inside his filthy clothes. Not many of the one percent thought bath time need be a regular occupation, but Snake took it to a whole new level, like he figured soap might lower his chances of staying alive.

"I got no time for this. I'm calling it. Hunter, you're up to bat." He added a smug death head grin.

Fuck. An hour before showtime and the game plan changes. Drastically. Now how was he going to keep all the balls in the air and not take the hit for it? This was his one chance to get out, make something of himself. The man had said he had talent, that his songs had real heart that Nashville would pay top dollar for. He could taste his longing and desperation to join the likes of Willy, Waylon, and Kris in the back of his throat making him swallow against the bitter bile. Outlaws and their songs that would stand the test of time. To continue with this fucked up arrangement was a death warrant, sure as shit.

"You got a problem with that?" Prez asked, his blank eyes not giving any quarter. Should have called him soulless.

"Nah, I'm good." He screwed down the hatch on his seething emotions like he'd been doing more and more often of late.

"Okay then. I want everyone keeping their eyes peeled for

those fuckin' Rebels and if you catch one alone, send a strong message and kick him to the curb. We clear?"

"Sure, Prez," Snake said, eying him sideways.

Hunter gave Snake a cold stare then walked away. Hopefully soon he'd never have to see his slimy mug ever again. Or any of them for that matter. Altamont had taught him a valuable life lesson, just not the one Prez spouted. A true outlaw lives his creed, not by hiding among thieves and killers under the guise of a so-called brotherhood, but by living free and making his own choices. Five years in this life was enough. He'd seen it all. Had a song catalogue to prove it. A sense of impending doom he tried desperately to shove away ate at him, driving his every action. Any slipup now came under penalty of death, either from this ruthless crew or the state. He wasn't sure which would be worse. At least a club's bullet to his brain was quicker than years dying inside another cage.

Sweet Cheeks flashed in his side rear vision and his feet took on a life of their own, headed her way.

"Fancy meeting you again, Hot Stuff," she said, her rosebud mouth pursed as she hid a smile.

Her friends both frowned but remained silent.

"So, what do you do besides strut around in gang colors?" she asked.

"Write a little music," he said. "In fact, one of my songs is going to be played tonight. 'California Outlaws.'"

Her brows rose in disbelief. "You write songs?"

"Yeah. What's wrong with that?" First time he mentions it to a female and he receives this sceptical reaction? Made him wanna keep on walking.

"Aw, sorry, you just caught me off guard. Wasn't expecting that. Can you sing me a couple of lines?"

"Nah, I have to be going."

"Don't be like that, Hot Stuff. I said I was sorry. I wish I could write songs. In fact, do anything creative." She smiled in a way that made anything she said downright forgivable.

"Goldie, don't encourage him. You dad's going to be mad enough as it is you snuck out," one of her friends spoke up, rolling her eyes.

"My dad can suck lemons," she said.

"Who's your dad?" Goldie. What a perfect name for her.

"He's only like Senator Spalding," the friend said with a smug smile.

Shit. Just his luck.

"Nice meeting you, Miss Spalding," he said and smartly walked away. Back on point, the change in vibe around him became apparent. Drugs and alcohol were flowing and the crowd was getting rowdier, some meaner, some looking like they were visiting la-la land.

"We want Waylon!" The chant was picked up by the entire venue, the noise drowning out the first musicians that had taken the stage. It was an eclectic group of bands playing tonight for charity, from hard rock to pure country. But if they wanted Waylon, they'd have to wait. The big headliner would end the show.

"Take that back!" a loud voice shouted nearby.

Hunter whirled around. Two half-drunk men were nose-to-nose not ten feet away. One shoved the other, spilling the man's beer all down his shirtfront.

"You bastard!" the second man raised a fist and slugged the other. The man stumbled backward but kept his footing.

"Fight! Fight!" the crowd roared, parting to give the contestants room to spar.

He dove in, got right between the sweaty red-faced men and raised his arms to keep the pair apart. "You're both going to have to leave if you don't settle down."

"Tell him to stop hitting on my woman," one of the men slurred, pointed at a well-endowed young woman in a narrow bandeau top and short shorts. She would look equally comfortable standing under a streetlamp down on Higgins and Main making a few bucks. Fighting over pussy, of course. Question remained, were they too drunk to see reason?

"What's it going to be? You gonna shake hands or do I have to sling your asses out of here? You'll miss the rest of the concert." He outweighed both of them by a good fifty pounds, all muscle from long hours spent in the gym, dreaming of a better life and knowing how slim his chances of ever escaping destiny. So bring it on. A good fight would help ease the aggression and desperation building in him since the Prez's edict. That game changer was the death card waiting to be played. God, he wished he was far away, given time to think it all through, not stuck in the middle of the action with no way out.

Both of them gave him a stupefied appraisal, swaying on their feet. Then a popular new song poured out over the crowd and the girl in question turned her back on them and began dancing to the driving beat. She was good, he'd give her that. Everyone took a full five seconds of their too short lives to admire her tight ass wiggling in the shorts.

"We're fine. Right, Rodney?" One offered his hand to the other combatant.

"I love you man," Rodney said. "She ain't worth it."

Hunter left them to their romance and headed for the can. Needed to see a man about a gun. But just before he made the doorway marked GENTS, the music stopped.

"Tonight, the Wildmen have a special treat for Nashville. An up-and-coming songwriter by the name of Hunter Knight wrote the song 'California Outlaws' and we're going to sing it for y'all for the very first time on stage." The familiar melody broke out, nailing him to the spot.

The heart's a lonely hunter when running's all you got,
At a little border town when midnight struck and taught,
No law left unbroken,
No man without a gun,
My outlaw days are over if she would look my way,
The moment gone I reckon for me to have my say,
No law left unbroken,
No man without a gun,
The heart's a lonely hunter when running's all you got.

The crowd had gone silent. His spirits dropped along with the lack of noise into his scuffed leather boots he'd vowed to die in. Was today that day? Was his number coming up on the big wheel? He didn't bother waiting for the second verse of the song that seemed written a lifetime ago, and slipped inside the darkened doorway to retrieve the revolver.

The Saturday Night Special was still taped behind the tank where Hunter had deposited it earlier. He yanked it out and removed the final bits of black electrical tape before placing it at the small of his back, tucked in the waistband. Fate was calling his name. Damn it, but he could write a slew of songs about Goldie. Too bad she's a senator's daughter and not for the likes of him.

He exited the stall, glancing in the overhead mirror. Squinted his eyes at the solemn image of a desperate guy reflected back. *It's showtime, buddy.*

The British group that had scorned the club so publicly this past month was just making the stage when he strode up. Only a few minutes left before the die was cast and no going back. He could hear the rapid beat of his own heart, the intake and exhaling of every breath. Alive. But for how long? No way this could work out.

"Hunter, there you are," Buck Wilson said, hurrying over to join him. He was backed by his band that fanned around him while he spoke. "I just had to tell you the good news. It couldn't wait. Your 'California Outlaws' is headed to airplay. We recorded it earlier today on our latest album by the same title. Should be in the stores in a matter of days. You're going bigtime, buddy, what you got to say to that?"

Stunned, Hunter actually had nothing to say to that. It was too rarified an atmosphere, too far for what he was being called upon to do now. Heaven does not co-exist right next to hell for a reason.

"We've got a bus with your name on it. You can leave this gig tonight, with us. Just say the word. Leave the colors behind. Join with the real outlaws."

Huh. Well, he'd be dinker damned. This was a touch more than unexpected. A small ray of light opened at the end of the tunnel before it slammed shut again. He was in too deep now. It was too late, far too late.

"I don't want to get you guys in trouble with the club. The Prez doesn't take kindly to bands dishing us or getting in the way. Probably best I wait a bit, get out later. Then you won't be blamed." That's if he wasn't sitting on death row. *No, I won't let them take me alive.*

"*Phttt.* We can take it. We're not pussies like that British rock band. We're good ole boys, can handle a hit and keep on truckin'. You change your mind, join us at the bus. We'll be leaving shortly." Hunter shook Buck's hand and thanked him.

He turned his back on the best opportunity of his life, the only way out of his cage and looked toward the stage, his brain hurting from the pressure. Time was up.

"Hey, Hot Stuff, I'm sorry about my friend. She shouldn't have told you about my father."

Inwardly, he groaned, and looked up at the heavens. What's the deal tonight? *You just can't let it alone.* What would Sun Tzu say about that? Right. *The supreme art of war is to subdue the enemy without fighting.* Not that he wanted to fight with Goldie, far from it.

"It's a rather important fact, don't you think, your dad being a big time politician? Best forget we ever met."

"But I was wanting a ride on your Big Boy. You promised me. And a gal can't help who her father is."

Neither could he, except his deadbeat dad was a layabout who tortured his wife and kids just for the hell of it. But the downturn of her mouth when she mentioned her daddy suggested he wasn't one of her favorite people either.

"I'll take you for a ride, okay, just not now. Things are in play. Dangerous things. Best if you rejoin your friends."

She frowned, made a cute pouty expression. "I enjoyed your song by the way. You got real talent, Hunter Knight."

He liked the way she said his name a little too much, like it already had star power. But then a chill skittered down his spine when he caught Prez glaring at him. The asshole who called himself a leader made a nod at the stage with his head while drawing a quick line across his throat. Crap. The band was just finishing up a tune. Past time to wrap this disaster up. If he didn't complete the mission, it would be him laying in an unmarked grave before sunrise.

"I need you to leave now. Whatever you thought might happen here, it's not going to, okay? My fate is set and you can't be part of it. Just go."

Her blue eyes filled with tears and she swiped at them, half-shouting over the din of music. "Fine. Not like I can't find another man with a heart—no, make that heartbeat."

The crowd fever was building into a swaying sea of faces, the hard music on stage giving no relief as the group sailed into their signature song. Didn't look like any of them were going to get any satisfaction tonight. Besides, Hunter far preferred a country ballad any day of the year.

As Goldie hustled away, he was jostled by the crowd. Unusual, because his size and demeanor usually meant most people gave him a wide berth. A lot of glazed looks met his view when he gave a quick appraisal of the crowd. Damn, the LSD and magic mushrooms were kicking in. Fast. Looked like the entire venue was spinning out, ready to reach for a higher level of consciousness if Timothy Leary was to be believed. Sun Tzu would not approve.

"*I can't get no-oh-o satisfaction,*" one of the revellers sang off-key in his ear. He gave the man a gentle push away. Then a hand from the opposite side grabbed at his, and the whole crowd linked arms, swaying to the beat. *Holy fuck.* How was he supposed to do his job now?

Of all songs to consider a kumbaya song, this one got picked? He obviously couldn't pull the trigger until the crowd let go. He didn't want to hurt one of them, just do what had to be done since there was no other choice if he wanted to continue breathing. And his lungs would prefer that option. His heart too. Maybe it would be best to head backstage, do it there? Yeah, that might work.

Hunter nodded at Prez that he was still onboard. The look of frustration on his president's face was priceless, held in the same grip as everyone else. He pitied anyone having to stand next to Snake, the stench would send them reeling into hell, not rising to heaven. But the club was supposed to rally around the shooter, make it harder to tell who fired the shot while others set off fireworks at various locations as a distraction. Not happening now.

As the song concluded, the band bowed and deserted the stage. His fellow music fans let go of his arms. He bolted for the stage, hit the stairs two at a time, gained purchase on the top step and dashed into the wings. Mere seconds left before time ran out. His boots echoing on the wooden floor, he ploughed straight into another body blocking his path.

"Hold on, Hot Stuff, no need to bowl me over. You had me at riding your Harley."

What the hell was Goldie doing here? Right, the lanyard with the backstage pass hung around her neck. Over Goldie's shoulder he caught a glimpse of the backs of the British band as they vanished out the rear exit while he struggled to keep her upright. The distinct sounds of a helicopter's rotors firing up sent his adrenaline into overdrive. They were leaving and he was about to lose his chance. His life wasn't worth a plugged nickel if he didn't finish this.

"What's the matter? You look like you just saw a ghost."

"Yeah, *mine* if I don't catch up with the band that just left the stage."

"What do you mean? That's crazy talk." She clung onto him and wouldn't let go. He tried to pry her off, but she was having none of it.

"I got a job to do. Best let me go." Hunter sensed the wrath of Prez and the others right through the thin black curtain that separated them. Killers on one side of the line, what waited on the other?

"No, not until you tell me what's going on." She held on tighter, her arms and legs wrapping around his. She was no timid wallflower. It would be funny if it wasn't so tragic.

The sounds of the helicopter rising told him it was over. Too late. Death's sharp sickle hung over his head now, about to descend.

Defeated, he gave her a lopsided smile. "Well, we'll never know now. They're gone."

"The band. You were supposed to do something to them?" Her blue eyes sharpened.

"No matter."

She slid down off his body and regained her feet. He had to say having those luscious assets pressed up to his was by far the sweetest, most poignant moment of his entire existence. At least he'd exit this earth having had one glorious moment with a gold dust woman.

"What are you going to do now?"

"Not much for it. The club will be gunning for me. You should leave. Stay safe."

"I can't leave you here like this! What about your music? You got a gift to share with the world. Come, I know a way out of here." Her pretty face filled with an earnestness that damn near broke his heart. If he had one left after the shit he'd seen and been through. Soon enough it would give its last beat. Probably only minutes away.

"No, I can't let you get involved. It's too dangerous." He heard footsteps just then, pounding up the staircase that led to the stage. He had to get her to leave, she was in danger, how could she not realize that?

She grabbed his hand. "Come on. We can do this. Let me help."

If he couldn't get her to leave, he had to do something. Anything. "No. I have a better plan."

Hunter ran full bore dragging Goldie along with him, her feet barely touching the ground. *Where was it?* The parking lot behind the stage was filled with tour buses and roadie equipment trailers. What he needed to see wasn't in sight. Was it too late? They raced down the rows of vehicles while he prayed for a break.

"You can take the limo with me. Lots of room," Goldie said, her voice trembling from all the running.

There it was. The glory bus with WILDMEN scrawled along the side in big bold letters.

"No, I got something better. I got offered a ride on that bus." He pointed out the big brown and gold metallic vehicle.

Her eyes widened. "The Wildmen. Cool."

"Come with me," he urged, sharing a grin. "Lots of room aboard the Big Boy."

"I believe my agenda is open this week, so, hell yeah!"

They clamored up the stairs, the door closing behind them with the hiss of hydraulic cylinders. The driver let out the clutch, and the bus began to move ahead.

"Just in time. We were hoping you might join us. Don't want a repeat of Altamont, right?" Buck said. "And who's this lovely young thing?"

"Goldie Knight," she said before I could answer. *What the fuck.* She had lady balls, he'd give her that. Then again, she probably didn't want to make mention of her father at this moment. The band might throw them both off. Outlaws don't think much of scummy politicians and is there any other kind?

"You didn't tell us you were married, Hunter. Congrats. We'll bust open a magnum of champagne to celebrate the occasion. Plus, not everyday a songwriter joins the big leagues."

"We're not. We just share the same last name," Goldie corrected them, giving Hunter a wink. Sure, she owned her shit.

He glanced out the window, relieved to see the glass was tinted and no one could know they were aboard. Especially since he caught sight of Snake creeping along using another bus as cover, obviously looking to track him down, still looking green around the gills. But the guillotine blade had stalled, hovering just over his neck with indecision. It looked like he might get to live another day. He took a rare deep breath.

Who knew what lay down the road? The path in the woods he'd chosen maybe the one least travelled, but the Prez prided himself on no unfinished business. And Goldie, she was a senator's daughter. When the running got too hard, she'd bail. Hadn't everyone else in his life?

But for now, he had a song to write: "The Outlaw and the Lady". Or "What the Hell is She Doing Hangin' With Me?" Or anything really, to keep his mind off the punishing weight of his former life holding him down. Hmm, it was the human condition really, this building of cages, this suppression by others to save face. We are the result of unnaturalness, like animals who chew up their own legs or lick off their fur from worry. Only cages can do that.

Damn it, I'm missing out on Waylon's set. It made him want to bust someone in the chops, for only a fellow outlaw could understand where he was coming from.

Goldie laid her hand on his arm, like she could read his dark thoughts. That thousand-watt smile that could light up any life pressed against him. Warmed him. Yes, he would try to keep clear of cages from now on. Try to keep the door slammed shut against his former life. Because just maybe it was a woman who would save him, at least for a while…

Mom prayed for him, and prayed at him,
but didn't let him back in when the prayers didn't take.

Burke De Boer

People in Dallas Got Hair

Pop grew up on a farm in a town called Poetry, and supposedly it was a pretty place before the bank took it. Didn't do Dermitt a whole lot of good, growing up in South Dallas.

Pop used to rattle on about it. They bought colts and fillies young and trained them up and sold them as performance horses to ropers and cutting riders and every so often even barrel racers, even though barrel racers were, according to Pop, "a bunch of uppity bitches. So are ropers, of course, hell, ropers even more so."

Pop and Grandad and Uncle Chris would run the topic over and over again, whenever they went up to visit Grandad in his trailer in Sherman. Grandad never drove into Dallas.

"Well sure they're worse," Grandad would say, about the ropers. "'Cause a man should know better." Every time they brought it up it was like dragging pasture: rehashing the same old shit, and agreeing on the same old thing. That the only rodeo cowboys worth a damn were the roughstock, but the only ones worth any money were the timed event riders.

Dermitt spent most of his time on these trips looking off toward the Red River horizon, across the rooftops of the neighbor trailers, and listening to the roaring sounds of the county speedway which was just around the corner and up the road. He never rode a horse, much less roughstock. From a young age, he did work on cars though. When all was said and done, the trips to visit Grandad were mostly exercises in patience, and the older he got, the harder the visits were to sit through.

Late July 1990 was one of the most excruciating. Dermitt was fifteen then, and his kid brother was tagging along on these trips to Sherman. Grandad's place was well-lived-in, and he was running a gun repair shop out of the garage he'd built on. Boxes of stocks and sights and firing pins were littered all around the carport and the kitchen table. And Waylon's album *The Eagle* came out that year.

Pop played it in the tape deck, all the way through on one side, all the way through on the other, and back again. He took the long way home, so they could go through Poetry and see the old farm, so he could say "Yup, they're growing soybeans. Just like I told him: soybeans and corn, that's the way farms are going, you just cycle 'em through every few years. Soybeans and corn." And then he would hyperfixate on the song "Where Corn Don't Grow," and he got pretty damn good at timing the rewind on the cassette so he could back it right up to the start as soon as the song finished.

That was the last time Dermitt went to Grandad's before he went to prison.

"Juvie" would be what anyone who actually did time would call it, but Dermitt thought it made him sound harder to say he went to prison. What the hell else can you call an East Texas state school anyway, if not a prison?

After his first year, they offered him to play on the football team. Since the gun he stole was his Grandad's, and the car he stole was just a parked one and not a full-on jacking, he was considered nonviolent. And having served a year, his sentence was half over. This made him one of about twenty-five eligible kids to field the team.

Rusty loved football, the little squirt, and had always begged Dermitt to play with him, going on for minutes which felt like wretched hours. They didn't have much of a front yard, and the back was filled up with four mechanic's special project cars, so as Rust grew they had to move their practices out into the street. Goddamn if that boy wasn't getting good at booting it down the road either. Their spot in Dallas was on a dead-end, just before the asphalt turned to mud. First Rusty got good at kicking it so that it didn't hit any cars parked on either side. Then he got strong—kicking it way up high, sailing end-over-end past the stop sign, past the cross street where the left turn took you past a whole block of black families to the Confederate Memorial Cemetery and the right turn took you past a whole block of Mexican families to the tire shop and its adjoining Straight Razors Motorcycle Club headquarters, which was home to their own confederate flag.

Maybe Dermitt had too much of Pop's sentimentality in him, but he couldn't think of football without thinking of Rusty, so he told the coach no. He kept at work in the machine shop.

He came out of the joint even better at engines than he went in, and had learned to weld, and all things considered, was prepared for the world he wanted to live in. This included the tattoo etched into the side of his hand with a secretly whittled stick-and-poke. A St. Peter cross, like their last name, not an "inverted cross" tribute to Satan or whatever shit the dumbass kids in the state school and the halfway house thought.

And then he was back, and glad to be. The old project cars in the backyard had been cycled out and replaced with new project cars. "Sure, made some good money," Pop nodded as they stood together on the back porch. It didn't have an awning anymore and the freezing rain of January drummed on their hat brims and the cold wind froze their nose hairs. "If we can't break horses no more, might as well break cars."

"How about motorcycles?" Dermitt asked.

"I've been a pickups and cars guy my whole life, wouldn't know where to start."

"We can figure that shit out. I fixed up tons of lawn mowers and leaf blowers in the joint."

"In the joint, huh?"

They laughed, but Pop's might have been a cover for a scoff. Dermitt hardly noticed. Looking at something right in front of him made him feel alive. A thing to dial in on, it focused him on the present and the future. He couldn't take the goat-eyed navel-gazing of staring into middle distance; the fuzziness of the past which settled unfocused on the horizon line. Pop could reflect and worry and contemplate all he wanted. Anyway, Grandad had died while Dermitt was in his minor league prison and there were no more trips to Sherman. The old man's old man finally did make a trip to Dallas, and it was expressly to die in a hospital and leave the family with more bills on top of their bills. But after it all, *The Eagle* was still on rotation on Pop's tape deck.

Rusty had done so good on his middle school football team and on his middle school test scores that the parish school was offering him free tuition. Pop even got in good standing with the church to help make it happen. Of course, Mom had been in good standing this whole time. Rusty always was more of his mama's child.

"So, the St. Peters are going to St. Jude's," Dermitt assessed and couldn't decide if he felt pride or pity. "You gonna go pro?"

"I don't know."

"Seeing 'Rusty St. Peter' on the draft board would make up for all the kids saying you got a Rusty Peter, huh?"

"It's Rustin now."

"Right. Eighth grade. You're grown up." His tone straddled between apologetic and sarcastic, which was as close as he ever came to saying sorry. Despite being a grown-up eighth grader, he noticed that Rustin did have a copy of Waylon's new kiddy-song album, *Cowboys, Sisters, Rascals & Dirt* beside the boombox on his desk. He picked it up and looked it over.

"Dad got me that," the kid said.

Dad? Not Pop? "Yeah."

While Dermitt had been bunking continuously since Rusty got old enough to sleep in a bed, and then through the whole state school and halfway house, the kid had taken two and a half years off having a roommate. He didn't take kindly to the adjustment, naturally.

"Wake up, you're snoring."

"Shut the fuck up, I'm sleeping."

"You shut the fuck up."

And then, in a flash, Dermitt was on his feet and Rustin was flying across the room, crashing into the desk and sending all its contents flying. This included the boombox, which smashed to pieces against the floor.

Pop always said you gotta put the fear of God into a horse before it put the fear of God into you. It was the only way.

*

"Dermitt, wake up."

"Hmn?"

"Someone's at the door, get up."

"Erngh?"

She hit him with a pillow. "Answer the door!"

"Ah shit."

Ever since he became a half-patched prospect of the Straight Razors, Lamonta had gotten damn skittish. Dermitt thought this was goofy because they met at a party where he was a hang-around, so she should know they didn't mean anything with the rebel flag stuff. What would they be doing at so many race-mixed parties if they were supposedly as white supremacist as the Angels and the Gypsy Jokers? And why was she cool with them at the parties, but not at Dermitt's front door? She knew, he had told her time and again, what she was getting into.

Then he heard a clatter in the kitchen. Someone was coming in through the window.

He got his .45 out from the bedside drawer. His bare feet went silently across the bedroom carpet, and only tapped whispers across the hallway linoleum. The overhead fans spun lazily in every room in the house, and outside the cicadas sang their screaming nonsense into the night. All the sounds of sweltering heat covered the soft tip-tap of the balls of his feet sticking with every step as he crept down the hall.

He could only make out the movement of shadows over shadows, but someone was coming in through the window. And they were knocking shit all over the place coming in over the kitchen sink.

"Back up, motherfucker," he commanded.

"Ah, God," the shadow groaned, and he knew the groan.

"Rust?"

The shadow spat on the floor.

"God damn it, kid." He turned the light on.

"Agh, no, turn that off!" Rustin shielded his eyes.

"What the hell you doin', comin' in here?"

"Can you turn that light off?"

The leather arm of his letterman jacket was hiked up, but it seemed like the kid couldn't hike it up any further. He was turned away from Dermitt. It occurred to Dermitt that the kid wasn't just covering his eyes—he was covering his face. The body of his jacket was the deep maroon of the St. Jude's Academy Crusaders. But behind the gray leather which corresponded to the Crusader silver, a brighter red dripped onto the linoleum tile.

"What happened?"

"Can you just…" The kid peeked up and flashed the top half of his face, splattered with blood.

"What the hell happened!"

"I just need to wash up."

"Ya think? Yeah, come in here, we got shit in the medicine cabinet." He set the gun on the kitchen table. "And give me your coat, you don't want it all bloodied up. How the hell are you wearing a coat anyway? Was a hundred today."

Gingerly, Rustin pulled the jacket off. He had broken school records with punting in his career, and fielding punts too, and got to stay maroon even as he was bound for A&M, down that long road which calls itself I-45. He was a week away from reporting for training in C-Stat. But it was a chore getting the jacket off, his whole body beaten tender, and when it was off Dermitt saw he had no shirt underneath it, just a smattering of swelling bruises and bleeding cuts.

"What the hell happened," he repeated, gruffer, as he swiped the jacket. "You get thrown from a car or somethin'?"

"Yeah, let's go with that," the kid grumbled and went slinking off to the bathroom.

Dermitt headed down the hall after him and met Lamonta peeking out of the bedroom door. It wasn't a long hallway by any measurement, and even at the opposite end of the kitchen she had to glare against the sick glow of the fluorescent light.

"Who is it?" she whispered.

"Don't worry about it, baby."

"I'll worry if you don't tell me."

"It's just Rust. He got fucked up."

Her glare melted upward into a concerned furrow. "What happened?"

"You think this kid would tell me shit?" he said, and it was in response to her but directed at him. He stepped into the bathroom. Rustin was clearing out the medicine cabinet and under the sink. He had some rubbing alcohol and Band-Aids and rolls of bandages out.

"You got any gauze? Or can I use the bandage rolls without gauze?"

"I look like a fuckin' doctor to you?"

Rustin laughed, but it might have been a scoff.

"I got some," Lamonta said and tied her robe close as she walked to the kitchen.

Dermitt pulled the little bottle of Black Velvet out of the medicine cabinet and took a swig. He set it on the sink counter and said, "This'll help too."

Rustin grimaced. "I don't think it will."

Dermitt took the gauze and more wraps from Lamonta then closed the door. He took the Band-Aids too and sat on the edge of the tub and said, "Before I give you any of this you gotta tell me what happened."

He sighed. "I was at a party."

"Catholic school party?"

Rustin scoffed. This time it was unmistakable. "A neighborhood party."

"Aw shit."

"Don't worry about me."

"Bullshit I won't worry, hoss. If someone come after you, knowin' who you are, knowin' where you're goin', it's because they want to send a message to me. And the Razors."

"Can you fucking not? It's not all about you. You're not the king shit of Dallas."

This outburst was a weird response. Rust was the neighborhood hero with a big leg and an even bigger head. Punter, kicker, running back, sometimes strong safety. Track stud. When Pop got crushed by the eighteen-wheeler on I-35, they found his will written on a livestock bill of sale inside his floor safe. It left the working pickup—which had made all the Sherman trips—to Rustin, and the broken down ones in the backyard to Dermitt. Pop never bought Dermitt a car in his life, or dragged his ass back to church to get him into the good schools. Mom prayed for him, and prayed at him, but didn't let him back in when the prayers didn't take. The two brothers were a Crusader and a convict. By Dermitt's point of view, of course it wasn't all about him. Hell, it never was.

"Sure, it's not about me, all right, maybe it's about you. What happened, what'd you do?"

"Can I get those bandages?"

"Nope. You can swig that Velvet, though."

Rust did, and coughed. "Okay, I was at a party, we drank a little, we got into a wreck. I didn't want to cause a fuss with Mom…"

"You wanna keep fuckin' with me, asshole! Where's your shirt, huh? Those sure look like razor cuts on your body there, not no traffic accident."

He took a bigger gulp of Black Velvet. "All right. Yeah, I got beat up."

"By what army?"

"Just by some guys, I don't know."

"Who were they, what'd they look like?"

"Just some guys, they were just there."

"White, black, brown?"

"All of the above, a fuckin' Neapolitan."

"Huh?"

"The ice cream." He sighed and gripped the counter. "Can I get those bandages?"

Dermitt handed them over. "What'd they say to you?"

"Just that I was a weak-ass white boy."

"I thought you said one was white."

"Well, you know, a Slim Shady wannabe."

Dermitt scratched his beard and combed his mustache off his upper lip with a thumb and middle finger. "What are you gonna tell Mom? I'll let you stay here tonight, but you do gotta face her at some point."

"I don't know. Is my story working on you?"

"You're about halfway there. I guess she might buy it more than I do, though."

He sat in silence while the kid patched himself up. It was a long, slow, wincing process.

"I got some pain killers, too. Bottom shelf."

He found the pill bottle. "How many should I take?" he asked, already looking at the directions.

Dermitt grinned. He couldn't remember asking that before ingesting anything in his life.

The kid washed a single pill down with Black Velvet. He finished taping up the cuts.

"Come over here," Dermitt said. "I'll get the cuts on your back." He felt very much like a gorilla then, cleaning and dressing his brother's wounds like the apes groom their tribal brethren. Usually if Dermitt or Rustin laid their hands on the other, it was for fighting or rassling. This level of care was so human it felt animal. He nodded when he was done, then slapped the kid upside the head for good measure.

"Hey," the pup barked.

"We ain't got a guest room in the Palace of St. Peter, but you can crash on the couch."

"Thanks."

Dermitt went back to the bedroom and crawled on top of Lamonta.

"You can't be gettin' on me when it's this hot," she said.

"We'll get an A/C, soon as I make this New Orleans run." People paid a helluva lot of money for drugs, but with the expenses it seemed like all he ever did was break even. He knew getting patched up would mean more cash though.

"What happened to Rust?"

"Got his ass kicked. By a lot of guys, it looked like." In fact, the razor cuts looked pretty much like the Straight Razors MC's calling card. But that couldn't be.

"He didn't tell you, huh?"

"'Course not."

They laid together, side-by-side, and let the fans cool them off as best they could. Beneath the sounds of the singing cicadas, Dermitt swore he heard the front door open and close.

He grumbled as he got out of bed. Lamonta was already asleep.

Up the hallway, he found the couch empty. The door was unlocked, and the kid gone. He turned to head back to bed. That was when he noticed the kitchen table, a little square piece with foldable legs that Mom and Pop used to bust out for extra counter space on Thanksgivings. He remembered he'd left his .45 on it. And he noticed that it wasn't there now.

*

Sometimes people just got to go their own way. Dermitt was at Christmas Eve mass, which is the one time of year he actually attended mass, and with all of the priest's lecture about love and acceptance he believed that was the verdict: folks are different, and do different things. Giving them the freedom to be different is about the only thing that true love could be, in his esteem. The freedom to go or to stay.

Most of the congregation didn't extract the same lesson. He knew it. And he was only down in Laredo to pick up a giant duffel bag packed full of snow, fresh for the holidays, promising a white Christmas in the DFW. And an even whiter Y2K, if everything really was about to crash. But he had to get on the road immediately.

He wondered if Mom really believed he worked on the road as a mobile mechanic. He knew Pop wouldn't have.

Or maybe he would. Maybe he only remembered the old man being wise and discerning. Memories can get a little over-fond like that. Dermitt figured that people's memories change the past. It turns their dead loved ones into what they want the dead to be, and the departed ends up representing whatever ideal the living needs them to in the moment. They did the same thing with Jesus. And Judas, too.

If nothing else, Dermitt had a nicer spot in Deep Ellum than any other St. Peter had in South Dallas, or Sherman, or, by his measure, even Poetry. Getting fully patched up really had made a difference. More of a difference than Catholic school, evidently.

The air was biting cold. Windchill beat against his jacket and skull-print balaclava at highway speeds. The farther north he climbed, the worse it felt.

A cop lit him up outside of Waco. Their own band of religious nuts had been blown to smithereens almost seven years prior. It was deep in the December night. As he drifted to the shoulder, he knew there was a midnight mass about to meet somewhere in town, even with their big Baptist church and big Baptist college looming over the highway. He wondered what would be worse, getting locked up in this shithole town or dying in it? At least dying in Dallas felt right. It felt like that was the place where Dermitt St. Peter was meant to die. Like all the Y-chromosome St. Peters before him. So, when the cop's little megaphone squawked, "Don't pull over on the highway! Take the next exit!" he figured, sure, buddy. Let's find us some answers.

Joseph S. Walker

WRONG ROAD TO NASHVILLE

The open mic crowd stirred a little uncertainly when Caleb took the stage. It happened every time. Audiences weren't used to a guy his size singing, the guitar like a toy in his big, calloused hands. He looked more like a professional wrestler than a country singer. The beard he'd grown over the last couple of years helped a little. He hadn't yet resorted to a cowboy hat.

He started with a soft, familiar number, "Amanda," letting them know there was a real voice coming from the barrel chest, picked things up with a fierce "Ring of Fire" to get them stomping their feet, then slid directly into an original, "The Girl Two Doors Down." It was the best thing he'd written so far, with some clever wordplay and a rollicking sing-along chorus, and when he was done the applause felt authentic. The only sour note was that Jess wasn't there.

Rondel had a beer ready for him. "Killed it tonight, big man," he said, clapping Caleb on the shoulder. "When you gonna head to Nashville, get famous?" He was gone, heading for a cluster of sorority girls at the other end of the bar, before Caleb had a chance to say that he was a long way from being ready for that.

He didn't like the *big man*, but he'd put up with it for the free brew.

He downed half the glass, his hand still shaking a little from the adrenaline, and checked his phone. There was a text from Jess. *Sry 2 miss it. Make it up to u? Door's unlocked.*

Caleb grinned and finished the beer. The night was looking up. He and Jess had been a little bit of a thing for a month or so. When she invited him over at night, it always meant he'd be around for breakfast. Sounded like a hell of a way to celebrate a good show. *On my way*, he responded.

His jubilant mood lasted right up until he walked into her living room and found her sitting on the couch. The guy sitting next to her had a patchy beard, a line of red skulls tattooed along each forearm, and a shiny black automatic pressed hard into Jess's side.

"Christ," the man said. "Big fucker, ain't you?"

Caleb stopped dead in the doorway. There were two other men in the room. The scrawny one jittering around in the entrance to the kitchen was pushing forty, but apparently hadn't modified his fashion sense since he was a teenager. He wore baggy satin shorts and an NBA jersey several sizes too large. The third man, standing in front of the curtains with his hands neatly clasped, wore a gray suit and a military bearing. He didn't have a visible weapon, but the granite in his eyes made Caleb more afraid of him than he was of the armed man on the couch.

Jess stared at the carpet. She didn't look up as the man beside her nodded at the chair facing him, inviting Caleb to sit. Caleb looked at the man in the suit again, then stepped forward and lowered himself slowly into the chair. "What the hell is this?" he asked.

"Relax," the man with the gun said. "You're just gonna do me a little favor, Caleb. It is Caleb, right?"

Caleb nodded. He kept trying to catch Jess's eye, but she wouldn't look up.

"You can call me Crimson." He held up his free hand, displaying the line of skulls grimacing and tumbling across the skin. Caleb's eyes flicked to the tattoos, then back to Crimson's face. He didn't otherwise respond. "First thing, we're gonna need your car keys."

Caleb fished in his pocket, came out with the keys and tossed them on the coffee table.

"Tapper," Crimson said. The man in the baggy jersey leered at Caleb, grabbed the keys and left the room.

"He stealing my car?" Caleb asked.

Crimson grinned. "Nah. Just stocking it up for your drive."

"What drive?"

"You're taking a package to Nashville for me."

Caleb raised an eyebrow. "I am?"

Crimson tilted his head at Jess. "You are if you ever want to get a sweet piece of ass off your girl again."

Caleb felt his shoulders bunch up.

"You ought to be flattered," Crimson said. "We were having lunch today and just happened to overhear her bragging to another waitress about the big, tough boyfriend who made her feel so safe." With his free hand he played with the ends of Jess's long black hair. "Said you'd do anything for her. So, here's your chance."

Jess did look up now. Her eyes were huge and unreadable.

Tapper came back, twirling the keys. He tossed them to Caleb. "All loaded up," he said.

Caleb looked at the man in the suit, then Crimson. "What did he put in my car?"

"Just a couple of duffel bags," Crimson said. "No reason for you to worry about what's in them. Tapper's going with you. You drop the stuff at a place in Nashville, pick up the payment, come back. Meanwhile, Boyle and me will be keeping honey girl company."

Caleb looked again at the man in the suit. Boyle's face gave nothing back.

Crimson continued. "Twelve hours or so, you're back here. We take our money, and you never see us again."

"Why don't you do your own driving?"

Crimson pulled his lips back, flashing crooked yellow teeth. "Let's just say things are feeling a little too warm lately, copwise. Not just the local clowns. We got staties after our asses. Be on the lookout. Can't be out and about in our rides." He sounded proud.

"So? Steal a car."

"More heat? Pass. Tag, big fella. You're it." Crimson's face hardened, and he tightened his hand in Jess's hair. She winced, and Caleb's muscles tensed. "I don't have to tell you what happens if you get bright ideas, right?"

"No."

"Straight there, straight back, and this is all over. I'm just a story your grandkids won't believe."

"He's got a guitar in his trunk, Crimson," Tapper said. He licked his lips. "Maybe he can play me a little song while we go."

Crimson opened his mouth, but it was Boyle who spoke. "Girl told us you had a show tonight." His voice was like his face, flat and cold. "Said you're not bad. Really trying to make a run at it."

Caleb tried to match the emotionless tone. "It's going okay."

Boyle nodded. "Tapper," he said. "He does anything to

annoy you, makes any kind of try, break the guitar. Put it under a tire and run it over." He looked at Caleb. "Extra incentive never hurts."

Tapper just giggled.

"One last thing," Crimson said. "Give Tapper your phone."

Caleb hesitated. Crimson screwed the barrel of the gun harder into Jess's side, and she whimpered and shot him an angry glance.

Tapper took the phone Caleb held out and dropped it into a pocket. He pulled a revolver with a two-inch barrel from the other pocket, showed it to Caleb, and winked.

"Good boy," Crimson said. "Now, Tapper's gonna call me from your phone, every hour on the hour. I don't hear from him, you know what happens."

"Yeah," Caleb said. "I know what happens."

"Guess that's it, then. You boys better get on the road. Unless you need to make weewee first?"

Caleb stood. On his feet, he towered over the seated Crimson, and for a second, he had an urge to simply leap forward and overpower him. Maybe Crimson would get startled and try to shoot him, instead of Jess. Maybe he could bowl the whole couch over backwards and come out of the scrum with the gun.

Boyle had unclasped his hands. They hung loosely by his side, and his eyes sharpened. He looked like a shortstop, ready for the pitch, ready to react to whatever happened.

"All right," Caleb said. "I'll do it. But you don't touch a hair on her while I'm gone."

"Caleb, buddy." Crimson put on an exaggerated look of pity. "Get used to this right now. There are people in the world who do whatever they want. And there are people who can't do shit about it. Why don't you think that over on your little road trip?"

*

Caleb's fifteen-year-old Honda sedan was a tight squeeze for him, but he'd picked it up cheap and it still ran fine. As he was easing his bulk behind the wheel, Tapper got in the back seat, on the passenger side. Caleb caught his eyes in the mirror.

"You're less likely to fuck around if I'm not up there with you," Tapper said. He made a show of fastening his seatbelt. "Get moving."

Caleb pulled slowly away from Jess's house. "I'm guessing I want the Interstate."

"Well, yeah. What way you usually go to Nashville?"

"I've never been there."

Tapper snorted. "I thought you were a fucking singer, man. How you gonna live five hours away from Nashville and never go?"

"I'm waiting until I'm ready. There's a right way to get there and a wrong way."

"That so?" Tapper was quiet for a few minutes as Caleb merged onto the Interstate. "Which way you figure this is?"

He thought about waiting until he saw a cop and then swerving back and forth across lanes, begging to get pulled over.

He thought about deliberately crashing, hoping he'd come out of it in better shape than Tapper.

He thought about the ways Jess might find to thank him if they got out of this.

He thought about faking engine trouble. Overpower Tanner, take his gun, and go back to rescue Jess. He pictured himself kicking in the door and spraying Boyle and Crimson with bullets. Jess's lithe body winding itself around him, calling him a hero.

He thought about stopping for gas and just walking away.

He thought about a lot of things, and just kept driving, the miles slipping past under the wheels.

Tapper was annoyed that the car radio didn't have Bluetooth so he could listen to the music on his phone. "Not even satellite," he grumbled. "Fucking CD player. When's the last time you bought a damn CD? Might as well have an eight-track."

"Sorry to disappoint."

He skimmed across the dial until Tapper made him stop on a station with the kind of modern country music heavy on rap breaks and crude tributes to women in denim. Caleb winced at almost every song. Tapper sang along with most of them.

It was late now, and there was little other traffic on the long stretches between towns, except for the big rigs Caleb passed. A couple of times Tapper twisted around in his seat and pumped his fist at the drivers, trying to get them to blow their horns.

When he wasn't singing, Tapper kept up a constant stream of nervous chatter, his legs bouncing and jerking around violently enough for Caleb to feel the vibrations in the front seat. Working for Crimson was sweet. Plenty of money and access to good shit. Always women around, even if some of them were fucking junkies. He had lucked out when he and Crimson met several years back as cellmates. Crimson was moving up in the world and taking Tapper along for the ride. The only problem was that fucking Boyle, so smug, always dressed up like a lawyer or some damn shit.

As long as Caleb grunted once in a while to show he was listening, Tapper would keep talking.

He didn't forget his check-in calls, though. Every hour he called Crimson, told him everything was fine. The second time he did it, he asked Caleb if he wanted to talk to Jess, then laughed and hung up before Caleb could answer.

Right after his third call, they stopped for gas. Tapper took the keys, went into the station and came out with two plastic bags jammed full of soda and snacks. "Should have knocked the place over," he said as they got back on the road. "They don't want you to know, but those cameras behind the counter usually don't work. Feel like a sucker paying those prices."

"So why didn't you?" Caleb asked.

Tapper ripped open a bag of chips, spilling several out onto the floor of the car. "You heard Crimson. The whole point of this is avoiding heat. First time we did this I took a guy's wallet in a parking lot. Thought Crimson was gonna beat me to death when he heard."

First time we did this.

Caleb aimed for casual. "How many of these trips you made?"

"Three or four."

His knuckles whitened on the wheel. "Any of those hostages end up getting killed?"

He cut his eyes to the mirror and couldn't read the expression on Tapper's face. "Don't you worry about it, fella. All those women are just fine."

He didn't say anything about the drivers. He also didn't offer Caleb anything from the bags.

The miles rolled on.

Caleb didn't think of himself as a coward. He'd been in his share of fights. The year before, a football player at the high school where Caleb worked as a custodian went after a teammate in the cafeteria with a knife. Something about a girl, Caleb thought, plus a head-scrambling mix of teenage hormones and god knows what chemicals. The kid was a monster for his age, well over two hundred pounds, but Caleb pulled him off and kept him down until the cops arrived, even though the kid slashed his arm a couple of times. The school gave him a certificate, and there was a little news coverage. For a few days he thought it might kickstart his singing career, but everything died down.

Point was, he wasn't a coward.

But gambling with Jess's life was something different. It didn't matter that they'd only known each other a few weeks.

Tapper's never-ending drone was becoming sandpaper on his skin. He kept driving, keeping the car at a steady three miles over the limit, watching the distance to Nashville, on the big green signs after every exit, shrinking down toward nothing.

As they got close to the city, they hit an increasingly bewildering tangle of interchanges and signs. He tuned back into Tapper's endless monologue to catch instructions. He had never had much of a sense of direction himself. He had a vague sense that they were somewhere north and east of downtown when Tapper finally had him take an exit and get on the surface streets.

Within a few blocks, Caleb knew where they were, even if he didn't know what it was called. Sagging chain-link fences around unmown lawns. Empty storefronts alternating with dollar stores and payday advance rackets. Lopsided shopping carts on the sidewalks, often next to figures huddled in sleep or psychosis against doorways. Small apartment buildings with cardboard tacked over broken windows. Maybe he'd never been here, but he'd lived here all his life.

Tapper directed him to a long road of abandoned warehouses and light industrial shops, and finally had him turn into the drive of a business with a big sign reading

HODGSON CONSTRUCTION. The chain-link fence around this lot did not sag. It was ten feet tall and topped with loops of razor wire. Halogen lights illuminated a two-story structure and a cluster of pickup trucks and panel vans, all with the HODGSON logo. Caleb stopped at the closed gate.

"There's a camera," Tapper said. "Hang on a second." He opened his door and stepped halfway out of the car, tilting his face to the camera and waving. There was a grinding noise, and the gate rolled away. Tapper got back in. "Park right up there, by the main entrance."

Caleb put the car where Tapper said, killed the engine, and sat back, suddenly aware that he'd been hunching forward over the wheel for most of the drive.

"Pop the trunk," Tapper said. "Let's go."

"I figured I'd wait here."

"Figured wrong. Let's go."

The two duffel bags on top of his guitar case were black, with no logos or markings. When he picked them up, at Tanner's direction, they were heavier than he was expecting. He slung one over each shoulder and stood back from the car as Tanner slammed the trunk hard enough to make the car rock on its springs.

"Now get this before we go in," Tanner said. "These fuckers are stone serious. They think anything is screwy, they'll put us both in the dirt and let God figure it out. So you just keep your mouth shut and do what I say."

"Fine."

Tanner slapped him on the arm. "You're halfway home, bigfoot. Follow me."

They were met at the door by a Hispanic man in a security guard's uniform with a gun hanging from each side of his thick black belt. He gestured them in and led them through a dark, empty reception area. In the hallway beyond, three other men waited. All three were casually dressed and had guns. A Black man with spots of white starting in his dark hair seemed to be in charge.

"Drop the bags," he said. Tapper nodded, so Caleb lowered the duffel bags to the floor.

"Hands on the wall," the Black man said. "Spread your legs."

This time Caleb followed directions without checking with Tapper. He felt hands patting him down, but he just stared at the wall in front of him. Between his hands was an ancient poster demonstrating proper procedure for safely removing asbestos. The tape holding it up was yellow. Somebody with a marker had carefully drawn enormous breasts and huge dicks on every person in the illustrations. Caleb wondered if the artist was one of the armed men searching him for weapons and wires. It seemed unlikely.

"Tapper, you fuck." The Black man's voice was weary. "How many times have you been told not to bring a gun in here?"

"Don't give me a hard time, Leon. It's been a long night. Slipped my mind." Tanner's voice was a whine.

"I ought to shove this thing up your ass and pull the trigger," Leon said. "You'll get it back when you leave. Maybe." Somebody tapped Caleb on the shoulder. "Okay, let's go see the boss."

Celeb pushed himself off the wall, picked up the bags, and followed Leon and Tapper deeper into the building. The other men stayed where they were.

Leon led the way around a couple of corners. Tapper trudged along behind him, his fists clenched. Caleb carried the bags, doing his best to be invisible. They came to a door that seemed no different than the others they passed. Leon knocked and went in without waiting for an answer. Tapper and Caleb followed him into an office considerably better kept up than anything else they'd seen in the building, with clean new carpet and fresh paint on the walls.

The woman sitting behind the large oak desk was probably on the north side of fifty and just on the south side of obesity, what Caleb's dad would have called a substantial woman. It was a little past five in the morning, but she had a thick cigar in the corner of her mouth and a tumbler of amber liquid at her elbow. She was working on a laptop computer, peering at the screen through thick eyeglasses. Her eyes brushed the men, passing briefly over each, and went back to the screen.

Leon and Tapper stood quietly, waiting. Caleb leaned against the wall, crossed his arms, and waited, suddenly very aware that he hadn't slept. He couldn't remember the last time he'd been up all night.

It was three or four minutes before the woman grunted and closed the laptop. She put the cigar in a heavy ashtray, drank from the tumbler, and looked at Leon. "So?"

Leon put the little revolver on the corner of the desk. "Tapper forgot his manners again."

"Now that ain't fair, Ms. Rivkin," Tapper said. "I been on the road all night and it just slipped my mind. You can see it's just an itty-bitty thing."

"You find yourself saying that to a lot of women?" Rivkin asked.

Caleb couldn't stop the smile that flashed briefly across his face. He was pretty sure the woman saw it.

Tapper didn't smile. "You got no reason to be nasty to me."

"Seems like you and your boss forget things a lot," Rivkin said. Her eyes went to the bags on Caleb's shoulders. "I hope you didn't forget how much stuff to pack. Again."

"That was a one-time slip. We made it right."

"Eventually. Leon, why don't you take Tapper on back. The two of you can make sure everything got remembered this time."

Leon nodded and gestured to the door. Tapper turned to follow, and Caleb pushed off the wall.

"I don't think you need your pack mule for this," Rivkin said. "Why don't you leave him here. It'll do you good to carry your own shit."

Tapper looked back and forth between Caleb and the woman. "Crimson told me to stay with this guy."

Rivkin smiled. "Crimson isn't here." She said *Crimson* the way Alabama fans Caleb knew said *Auburn*.

Tapper looked at Caleb again, then Leon, and found no help. With a theatrically suffering sigh, he held out his arms. Caleb slipped the bags from his shoulders and handed them over. Leon nodded at Rivkin and led Tapper out of the room.

When the door closed behind them, it got very quiet in the office. Caleb could hear some kind of big machine running somewhere in the building, a humming punctuated by occasional thumps. Rivkin leaned back and gestured to one of the chairs across the desk. Caleb sat down and rested his hands quietly on the arms.

"Drink?" the woman said.

"Little early for me. Been up all night and I have another long drive coming up."

Rivkin nodded. She picked up her glass and drained it. "I don't envy you spending time in a car with Tapper. Known him long?"

"What time is it now?"

She took a bottle from a drawer and filled the tumbler almost to the brim. "So I guess you've met his boss."

"Crimson. Yeah."

"Crimson." Rivkin's mouth pursed, and she shook her

head. "That little prick's name is Chester, for Christ's sake. Fucking pathetic when people try to give themselves nicknames."

Caleb didn't trust himself to say anything, so he kept quiet.

"Of course, in this business you have to work with a lot of assholes." Rivkin took a long drink. If the liquor had any effect on her, she didn't show it. She rolled the glass between her hands and looked at him. "I will say he comes by it honestly. His father was every kind of dick known to man. Ended up alligator food in some swamp down there."

Tapper's gun was still sitting on the corner of the desk. Caleb looked at it for a second, then back to Rivkin.

"Then there's Chester's sister. Another prizewinner, loves playing men for dopes. The two of them have this con they like to do where they get some sucker to do their dirty work by making her out to be a damsel in distress. Save me, save me, all that shit."

Caleb's mouth was dry. "That a fact?"

"God's truth." Rivkin took a smaller sip. "That's something my mother used to say. God's truth. Here, I'll show you." She picked up a phone from the desk, scrolled through it for a minute, and slid it across to him. "How's that for a family portrait?"

Caleb leaned forward and looked, without touching the phone. The picture had been taken at some bar. Crimson was talking to somebody not in the frame. One of his skull-ornamented arms was draped around Jess's neck. She was holding a beer and her mouth was open in laughter.

Caleb made himself breathe evenly. A moment from several hours ago came back to him. Crimson screwed the gun hard into Jess's side and she looked at him for a second, not with fear or pain, but with the flashing, instinctive anger at a joke taken too far. The anger of somebody being tickled a little more aggressively than they wanted.

Jesus, he was stupid.

"Why are you telling me this?"

She pulled the phone back. "Just making conversation," she said. "Now, what Chester—I'm sorry, what *Crimson*—does have going for him is Boyle. You met Boyle?"

"Briefly." It was all he could do to stay in the chair.

"Boyle, there's a professional." Rivkin nodded to herself. "Plays everything square. Doesn't hurt anybody unless he has to. You could do real business with a man like that, if Chester was out of the way." She picked up the glass again. "Of course, that would require something really going wrong for Crimson."

She put the nastiest spin yet on the word.

Caleb stood up. He paced to the door, put his hand on the knob, and stayed there for a long moment. Then he went back to the desk, picked up Tapper's little gun, and put it in his pocket. Rivkin sat with the glass cradled between her hands, watching him.

There was a knock, and once again Leon entered without waiting, Tapper trailing behind him. "Looks good," Leon said.

Tapper was still petulant. "Told you so. It's kind of insulting, you checking."

"No doubt," Rivkin said. She opened a drawer and tossed a fat manila envelope on the desk. "You going to insult me back and count this?"

Tapper snatched the envelope. He looked at her, then Leon. "Course not."

"Then I think our business is done."

"Soon as I get my gun back."

"Oh, no," Rivkin said. She opened the laptop again, put on

her glasses, and began tapping at keys. "I'm keeping that. Call it a penalty for not following instructions."

"That's not funny, Ms. Rivkin." Tapper looked like he'd been slapped.

"No, it's not." She was fully absorbed in the screen. "Leon."

Leon took Tapper's left elbow. "Time to go."

"No, look—" Whatever Tapper was going to say was cut off by a strangled yelp. He tried to jerk his arm out of Leon's grip but couldn't do it. Caleb couldn't tell what the Black man was doing, but there were tears springing up in Tapper's eyes. "Okay, okay!"

Leon let go. Tapper stumbled to the door, his right hand holding the hurt arm against his side. "I'm gonna tell Crimson about this," he said. "Treat me this way."

Rivkin didn't bother responding. Leon opened the door and gestured them through. They wound their way back through the building, Leon walking quickly, Tapper muttering as he opened and closed his left hand, Caleb, in the rear, seeing nothing but the skinny man in the ridiculous outfit.

The corridor with the asbestos poster was empty. The security guard with two guns wasn't in the front office. Leon unlocked the front door of the building and stood aside to let them pass.

The door clicked shut behind them. As soon as he heard it, Tapper turned and spit at the building. "Goddamn assholes," he said. "Arrogant old bitch. Time we found somebody else to sell to."

He walked toward the car, Caleb close behind. The sky in front of them was turning pale, the hesitant purples and oranges of sunrise beginning to creep up from the horizon.

Tapper was reaching for the car door when Caleb stepped up close behind him. He wrapped his huge right forearm around Tapper's neck, locked it in by grabbing his left wrist, and began to squeeze.

There was more fight in the little man than he expected. Tapper clawed at his arm and kicked back desperately, yells coming out of his constricted windpipe as weak wheezing. Caleb squeezed harder and leaned back, lifting the smaller man several inches off the ground. He closed his eyes and turned his head to the side to avoid the hands scrambling to find his face. When Tapper's movements started to weaken, he opened his eyes cautiously and watched the ear he could see go from bright red to purple to blue in the slowly growing light.

It was over fairly quickly, but he kept the hold on until his arms started to cramp. Tapper's body collapsed to the ground like a broken doll. Caleb looked around. Nobody was on the street. There was a Hodgson camera on a nearby lamppost pointed right at him, but nobody came running out of the building to stop him. He opened the rear door, lifted the body, and pushed it across the seats. He doubted Rivkin's tolerance would extend to leaving Tapper in her parking lot. He'd drop the body somewhere, at least several blocks away. It seemed unlikely that the Nashville PD would be dedicating many manhours to an out-of-state ex-con turning up dead in a neighborhood like this.

The manila envelope was on the ground, too. He dropped it on the front passenger seat and took his phone from Tapper's pocket. About twenty minutes until the next time Tapper was supposed to check in. He blocked the number Tapper had been calling. While he was at it, he blocked Jess's too.

The Hodgson gate rumbled back for him as soon as he pulled up to it. He was suddenly aware that he was famished.

He had the money. He had his guitar. He had the gun, but

he'd be getting rid of that soon. He took a deep breath. Nashville. There were apartments everywhere, after all. There were janitor jobs all over the place. There would be open mics, probably one on every other block.

It wasn't the road he planned to take, but he had arrived.

Everyone stood as still as a painting,
eyes wide and hands in the air.

John M. Floyd

THE DEVIL'S RIGHT HAND

"I don't know," Jack Curry said, when they stopped on the ridge overlooking the town. "This might not be such a good idea."

Della Morgan, sitting beside him on the wagon seat and holding the reins, didn't reply right away. Ahead and below them, maybe three miles west, was a cluster of buildings she had told him was called Longbow, and behind them in the covered bed of her mule-drawn wagon were most of her belongings and the merchandise she used in her business. Curry's horse, a small bay with a white patch on its forehead, was tied to the tailboard.

"We'll be fine," Della said, "if you just do what I tell you."

He wasn't so sure of that. Her plan had sounded good at first—God knows he needed the money, even if it was illegal. But the more he thought about it . . .

"That bank might be crowded," Curry said, rubbing his bad leg. "How can you be sure all those people will think I'm this . . . what'd you say his name was?"

"Roland Cash. They'll think you're him, all right. You scared the hell outa *me*, that's for sure."

That much was true, he thought. He remembered the shock on the grayhaired woman's face when they'd met on the trail late yesterday afternoon. He'd stopped beside a creek to make camp, she rolled up behind him in her old wagon with DR. MORGAN'S LINIMENT AND MEDICAL AIDS painted on the side, and when he turned to look at her she almost passed out. Only after she heard his Eastern accent and saw his limp did she calm down a bit. Finally, after introductions and explanations, it was she who suggested they share a meal and a campfire, and as they finished their meager supper Della told him about the outlaw named Roland Cash.

"You're a dead ringer for him," she had said, still clearly amazed. "I never saw nothing like it." She even had a picture of Cash, a folded WANTED poster she took from a bag in her wagon. "Except for that scar over your left eye, you two could be twins." She paused, then added, "Or could've been. Most folks think Cash is long dead, posters or not. But when they see *you*, they'll think different." When Curry reminded her that what she'd seen of Roland Cash was a poorly drawn pen-and-ink sketch, she snorted and said her memory damn sure wasn't a sketch: she and her late husband Howard, a sort of traveling doctor with questionable methods, had seen the famous outlaw themselves ten years ago, in Dodge. Cash had been cooling his heels in the city jail at the time, although she later heard he hadn't stayed locked up for long. "Believe me," she said to Curry, "if Wyatt Earp was scared of the man, the folks at the Longbow bank'll be making water in their pants when they see you stroll in."

The plan she'd cooked up along with their beans and coffee had sounded foolproof, but sitting here now in the mind-clearing light of day, staring down at the sleepy town in the distance, Jack Curry was having second thoughts. "You say this guy Cash is—or was—a killer, right? What if somebody in the bank pulls a gun? I bought one, belt and everything, because I'd heard everyone out here carries 'em, but I sure never shot anybody. Never *been* shot, either."

"Nobody'll try to shoot you," Della said. "Just seeing your face'll scare 'em out of their knickers, whether some of 'em think you're a ghost or not. You'll say you want the money, they'll hand it over, and me and Bessie here'll be waitin' for you by the back door. You'll hop in and hide in the back there under them blankets, and we'll mosey on down the road. If there's a posse later, it'll charge right past us. Nobody'll suspect an old woman in a medicine wagon."

He had to admit, it sounded reasonable. He adjusted the blond wig and eyeglasses she'd given him to wear in public up until time for the robbery, squirmed a bit in her late husband's white shirt and black suit, and held onto the seat for dear life as she clicked her tongue to the old mule and they rattled down the rutted slope toward the town.

"Should I try to look mean?" he asked her, between bumps in the trail.

"Save it for the bank," she said. "Mean wouldn't work anyway, in that getup."

They checked into the town's only hotel, a three-story wooden building next door to the Bank of Longbow, and a blond haired and black-suited man by the name of Bob Smith used one of his last five dollars to pay for two rooms on the second floor. He and Della had lunch at a back corner table of the hotel's café, after which he holed up in his room—it smelled like old cigar smoke—while she scouted the bank and the streets and alleys they would use for an escape route. That night he decided it might be too risky to be seen anywhere, even in disguise, so Della bought meals from a restaurant down the street and brought them to his room for supper.

They talked until ten o'clock, mostly about the infamous Roland Cash. According to Della, the man was a hero to some, a monster to some, and a mystery in every way. His name was almost certainly made-up—the old joke about him was, if you're Roland Cash, you're rollin' in cash—and no one knew where he'd come from or where he was based. What everyone did know was that he'd supposedly murdered a dozen men and robbed twice as many banks and other establishments over the past fifteen years. In fact, the newspapers had given him a nickname—The Devil's Right Hand—and it was said he liked it. As for his current whereabouts, some swore he'd been cornered and killed in San Antonio by Texas Rangers, some said he was still seen regularly in Tombstone, some said he'd moved to Mexico and was running an oceanside cantina there, some said he'd died in a shootout and cave-in at a mine in the Black Hills, some insisted he was holed up with a girlfriend in Virginia City and only surfaced when his money ran out. Nobody knew anything for sure, and Della didn't seem to care. Even the ominous nickname didn't matter to her. All she and Curry (a.k.a. Bob Smith) needed to know about Cash was his reputation. Finally, they turned to a discussion of their plan, and went over the details one by one. Della was visibly excited. Curry was confident but still reluctant.

"I never shot anyone," he said again, "and I don't figure to start now. You understand that? I even took the bullets out of my gun."

She shrugged. "Suits me. I already said you won't need to use it. But you do have to wear it and point it, and act like you might."

"How's this for a scary look?" he asked, demonstrating.

"That ain't necessary either. Just 'cause you ain't never heard of Roland Cash don't mean they haven't. I promise you, these people see your face, they'll do whatever you want."

"I just want their money," Curry said.

"You and me both. And once we're out of town and safe, we split it up, half and half, and go our separate ways. Agreed?"

"Agreed."

Della stood, smiled, and left to go to her room. Surprisingly, Curry slept like a rock.

The next morning, he missed breakfast just to be safe, and whiled away the hours until noon watching the back part of the town through the window of his room. Around lunchtime Della again brought him food, and they went back over the plan. She'd decided their getaway would be easier if they struck late in the day instead of early, so they sat together in the room and played cards until well into the afternoon, when Della finally rose from her chair, collected the wig and eyeglasses and clothes Curry had worn the previous day, wished him good luck, and left. Half an hour later he watched through the window as she steered old Bessie and the wagon out of its storage spot near the hotel—his horse was still in the livery stable—and into the street behind the bank and around the corner. From what he'd seen yesterday, he knew there was a narrow alley on the far side of the bank, between it and a squat, flat-topped railroad office. He checked his pocket watch. It was 3:40. Right on schedule.

He stood, put on his hat, buckled his gun belt, and left the hotel, and at exactly a quarter to four he pushed through the front door of the bank. He then drew his empty revolver and informed the shocked crowd and employees—in case they didn't know from their own eyes—that Roland Cash was back from the grave and here to make an unscheduled withdrawal of funds. No longer in disguise, Curry felt a pleasant sense of accomplishment as the familiar name and face commanded the obedience it deserved: everyone stood as still as a painting, eyes wide and hands in the air. Five nervous minutes later he had several thousand dollars packed into two bank-bags. He wished them all a fond farewell and exited through the back door.

Della was waiting in the alley as planned, watching him from high on the driver's seat of the wagon. Moving fast even with his limp, Curry handed the bags up to her and was preparing to climb up also when she pointed and said, "Push them barrels over to the door to block it." This was unexpected and took what he thought were precious seconds to do, but he did as he was told.

It was as he turned back to the wagon that he realized his mistake.

Della had her own revolver out now, cocked and aimed straight at his chest. "Hop aboard, Mr. Curry," she said. "Change in plans."

He climbed slowly up onto the wooden seat. "What the hell are you doing?" he asked.

"What's it look like? It's called keeping all the money for myself."

Carefully, the reins held in one hand and the gun in the other, she drove Bessie and the wagon around the corner and back to the shed behind the hotel. Then, still covering her former partner with her gun the whole time, she guided him back to the bank on foot, pushed aside the three barrels blocking the rear door, and entered the building. The town sheriff, a redhaired man with a bushy mustache, had just arrived through the front door when he saw them.

"My name's Della Morgan," she said to him, prodding Curry forward across the lobby with the gun barrel, "and I'm turning in a criminal. The Devil himself."

Stunned, the sheriff produced a set of handcuffs and snapped them on. "Roland Cash," he said, staring. "Everybody thought you was dead." He added, to Della: "Well done, ma'am."

"Glad to help," she said, and smiled. "I heard there's a two-thousand-dollar reward?"

At least a dozen times over the next half hour Jack Curry tried to tell Sheriff Edwin Dorsey he wasn't Roland Cash and that Della Morgan had the bank's money, and at least a dozen times he was ignored. If not for a young deputy named Perkins, that's probably the way things would've stayed.

"I dunno, Sheriff," Deputy Perkins said. He was sitting on a corner of Dorsey's desk, not twenty feet from Curry's cell. "Some of what he's saying makes sense."

"What do you mean?"

"Well, for one thing, where's the money he stole? This Mrs. Morgan says she recognized him and got the drop on him when she saw him running out of the bank alley—but she says he was emptyhanded. I've looked everyplace for the money and the bank folks are still lookin', and nobody's found anything."

"I figure he passed it to somebody in his gang, and they took off," Dorsey said. Then, after a pause: "You said 'for one thing.' What else doesn't make sense?"

"The fact that his gun was empty." Perkins picked up Curry's revolver from the desktop, spun the cylinder, and put it down again. "Plenty of bullets in the gun belt, but not a one in his Colt. That don't sound like a seasoned criminal to me."

The sheriff didn't respond to that. He turned in his desk

chair, thoughtfully smoothing his mustache, and studied Curry a moment through the bars.

"Besides," the deputy said, "I saw Roland Cash once myself, over in Hays. A few years back. I watched him walk down the street and I know he didn't have no game leg. Didn't have that big scar over his eye, neither."

Jack Curry, listening closely to all this from his cell, said, "He's right, Sheriff. I've had this scar for thirty years, and the limp too. Like I've been trying to tell you, my name's John Robert Curry—everybody calls me Jack—and I'm from Boston, Massachusetts. I just came west from St. Louis a month ago. I got robbed by bandits and I'm flat broke and I swear I never heard of Roland Cash till that lying Morgan woman told me about him on the trail when I met her, night before last." Talking fast, he covered the strange events of the past couple of days and added, "I heard you say you've got to wait till you get a wire authorizing you to pay her the reward, right? Well, I'm telling you, don't pay her, authorization or not. She's as guilty as I am. I did indeed rob your bank, but I'm not the only one, and I'm not the one who planned it."

During the silence that followed, Deputy Perkins cleared his throat and said, "There's something else, too, Sheriff. Old Milton Elwood here in town was there when Roland Cash was cornered at that abandoned mine near Deadwood a couple years ago, and he's always said Cash didn't make it out alive that day. A body was never found, but he thinks Cash is long dead."

The sheriff nodded. "I thought so too. But if he's really dead, why's there still wanted posters on every tree 'tween here and New Orleans? Why's there still a reward on his head?"

"'Cause nobody's certain of it. But Elwood sure is. You ever talk to him about that?"

Dorsey sighed. "No, but I guess now'd be a good time." He squinted through the grimy window, rose from his desk, walked through the door and outside, and called a name. Seconds later a small boy appeared, listened to the sheriff a moment, and took off down the dusty street. Dorsey came back inside and said, "I just sent Jimmy Norton to fetch Elwood. We'll ask him." Turning to Curry, he said, "As for your identity, what does it matter who you are, Devil's Right Hand or not, if you admit you committed the crime?"

"It matters because I'm guilty of robbery and not murder," Curry said. "I'll go to prison if I have to, but I'm not a killer like this Cash fella. I don't want to hang for things I didn't do."

At that, they all fell silent. Outside in the street, a horse whinnied. A large clock on a shelf behind the desk ticked away the minutes. The sun was almost down now, its light through the unbarred front windows painting yellow rectangles on the jail office's east wall.

"What about the blond headed guy you killed?" the sheriff said.

"The what?"

"After we locked you up and went back to look for the money, this Della Morgan lady told me she saw you arguing last night with the man she came into town with, yesterday. Signed his name Bob Smith at the hotel. Everybody saw the two of 'em together, around noon—and she said Smith later disappeared without a trace. Said you murdered him." Dorsey's face seemed to say *As if I don't already have enough to worry about*. "You got anything to say about that?"

Curry let out a breath. "She's lying, Sheriff, and I can prove it. That fella she's talking about was me, wearing a yellow wig and a suit of clothes she gave me so nobody'd see the man they thought was Roland Cash before they were *supposed* to see me, this afternoon at the bank."

"Is that so. And how exactly would you prove that?"

A knock at the door interrupted them. "Come in," Sheriff Dorsey shouted. His towheaded errand boy opened the door and reported that Milton Elwood hadn't come home yet from visiting his sick brother, but his wife said that when he returned she'd tell him the sheriff needed to see him. Dorsey nodded, tossed the boy a coin, watched him leave, and turned again to the prisoner. "Did you hear me? How would you prove Della Morgan's lying?"

"I'd get you to search her room, and her wagon out back. She's still at the hotel, right? She must be, if she's waiting for you to pay her the two thousand. If you search the room and the wagon you'll find the bank's money in one of those places, plus the wig and a pair of specs and a black suit and white shirt she gave me to wear."

"Just how would I know you really wore 'em?"

"There's a new soup-stain on the shirt pocket, from our lunch in the hotel yesterday."

"And how would I know the clothes wasn't yours the whole time, put there by you?"

"Would I own a blond wig? Besides, the suitcoat has Della Morgan's late husband's name—Howard—written inside it."

The sheriff hesitated, considering that. "And if I do find all this, what's in it for you?"

"Not much," Curry admitted. "But maybe it'd convince you that she fooled me into doing this, which should also convince you of who I really am. Then at least I'd be prosecuted for bank robbery and not for multiple murders."

The sheriff mulled on that a bit, exchanged a look with his deputy, and nodded. "All right. Do it, Perkins. I think he's the liar, not her, but I guess we can check it out. The money damn sure went somewhere."

"Yessir." The deputy socked a hat on his head and left.

When he was gone, Curry sat down on his bed, which felt as hard as it had looked. Sheriff Dorsey settled again into his chair, propped his boots on the desktop, and looked out the window. The clock kept ticking.

After a while Curry said, "This town have some kind of connection to Indians?"

"What?"

"Longbow. Sounds like an Indian name, to me."

The sheriff shook his head. "It started out Longbaugh. B-A-U-G-H. He founded the town. Name got misspelled on some document someplace, and it's been Longbow ever since."

"Good lord," Curry said. "You folks here can't get anything right."

Dorsey chuckled. "Says the man on the other side of the jail bars."

"I won't be, for long. You'll see."

"Yeah, we'll see, all right."

A silence passed. At last Curry sighed and said, "I didn't mean any disrespect, Sheriff. I'm much obliged to you, for doing this."

"Doing what?"

"Checking Della Morgan's room, and wagon."

Dorsey nodded, still staring out the window. Slowly he ran a hand through his red hair.

"Perkins likes doing that kinda thing," he said. "It ain't like he's busy otherwise."

An hour later Deputy Perkins came back. The look on his face told it all.

"I turned her room upside down," he reported. "The wagon too. No blond wig or suit or eyeglasses, and no money or bank bags. When I apologized to her, she just said to tell you to hurry up and get that reward processed so she can leave town."

Sheriff Dorsey shifted in his desk chair to gaze through the bars at his prisoner. "What do you have to say about that, Cash?"

Jack Curry felt his heart sink. His leg hurt, his stomach churned, his head ached. *How had she done it?* There hadn't been time for her to hide all that stuff, especially two huge moneybags. Where would she hide it, anyway, except in the room or the wagon?

Curry sat there on the edge of the bed, smelling the jailhouse scents of old brick and sweat and despair and staring through the window of his cell. Not that there was much to see there. Just the side of another building next door . . .

Then it hit him. *He knew what had happened.* The warm and sweet light of understanding flooded into his brain like the setting sun's rays through the office's front windows.

"I know where it is," he murmured.

Both Dorsey and Perkins gawked at him. "Where what is?" Dorsey said.

"Everything. My disguise—the wig, the clothes—and the bank's cash too. I know where you can find it all. Right now." He looked back at them and let another silence drag by.

"Well, then," the sheriff said, "where is it?"

"I'll tell you—if you'll make a deal."

"What kind of deal?"

Curry drew a long breath. "Let me go free."

"What?!"

"Just listen, Sheriff. If I don't tell you, you'll never get that money. The bank'll be out however many thousand dollars was stolen, and it's a lot. If I do tell you, and you find it, you'll also find the evidence I told you about—the wig and so forth—and you'll know she was lying about everything, and that I'm who I say I am. You'll be a hero, you can put Della Morgan in jail where she belongs, you can stop looking for the body of a blond-haired friend of hers who never existed, and since I'm not Roland Cash you'll save two thousand dollars in reward money that you would've otherwise paid her. Think about it: you'll have the bank robber who really plotted the crime." He paused. "I'm just a damn fool who got talked into playacting like a real criminal. I'd leave here broke, yes, but I'd also leave a free and changed man."

The room grew quiet. Once again, the sheriff and deputy looked at each other.

"But if you do this, if you go where I tell you to go," Curry continued, "it'll have to be right now, before it gets dark. After that, the money'll be gone."

"Why will it be gone then, and not now?"

"You'll see. Do we have a deal?"

Perkins was chewing his lip. "We'd have to talk to the bank manager first, Sheriff."

"No we wouldn't," Dorsey said, his eyes on Curry. "This has to be my decision."

More silence. Somewhere outside, a buckboard rumbled past. A dog howled. The sheriff's clock chimed the half-hour.

At last, he nodded. "You got a deal," he said. "Where's the money?"

This time both the sheriff and deputy went to look. And ten minutes later they came back to the jail with both bank bags in hand. Sheriff Dorsey carried the cash and Perkins had the wig, spectacles, and clothes. They dumped everything onto the desk.

Without pausing Dorsey turned, unlocked Curry's cell door, pulled it open, and watched him limp out into the office. "It was right where you said it was," Dorsey said. "On the edge of the roof of the railroad station, next door to the bank. How'd you know?"

"I didn't, for dead certain," Curry said. "But it's the only place it could've been. When I came out of the bank and gave her the money, Della sent me back to block the rear door with barrels from the alley. We hadn't planned for that—or at least I hadn't—and when I got back to the wagon, she had her gun aimed at me. She'd stayed on the wagon seat the whole time, and it's a tall wagon and the roof of the railroad building on the other side of the alley is low and flat. I know now she must've used the time that my back was turned to swing those moneybags up onto the roof—the alley's narrow so it wasn't much of a reach. She had probably already stowed the yellow wig and clothes up there while I was still inside the bank." He paused, thinking. "That's why she took the extra time to drive me and the wagon back to the shed behind the hotel before marching me into the bank to turn me in. She wouldn't have wanted the wagon sitting there in the alley where you might figure it all out, when you realized the money was missing."

Dorsey and Perkins sat stock-still, listening to every word. When Curry was done and the two lawmen had taken a minute to process it all, the sheriff said, "Why'd you tell us we had to go get it 'right now'?"

"Because I guarantee you Della will be going back for it herself, soon as it's full dark." Curry checked the window. "And it's almost that, now. If you want your other robber, you best get back up on that roof quick and wait for her."

Deputy Perkins took that assignment, and left in a hurry. And sure enough, he showed up a short time later with Della Morgan in tow. She hadn't been handcuffed—being female did have some advantages, apparently—but she was closely watched, and within minutes she had taken residence in the cell Jack Curry had just vacated.

Perkins's report was short and to the point: "I hid and waited behind a chimney on the roof till she climbed up there," he said.

Sheriff Dorsey nodded, studying Della's face. Everyone had fallen silent.

She glared at him, then pointed to Curry. "Why ain't he behind bars too? The whole thing was his idea."

The sheriff shook his head. "I don't think so. I now believe this man's no more the right hand of the Devil than I am. I believe he's who he claims to be, and even though I also believe he's dumb as a post in some regards and certainly committed a crime, he's getting a reprieve in this case."

"A reprieve?"

"Yes ma'am. A dispensation based on information he gave us leading to the recovery of stolen money, the solving of the so-called murder of the so-called Bob Smith, the prevention of an unearned reward payment, and the arrest of a fellow participant in a bank robbery. That decision could be argued, but it was my decision to make and I made it."

Everyone else in the jail, including Perkins, seemed surprised at this long speech, and stared quietly at the sheriff a moment. Della Morgan indeed looked ready to argue, but even she seemed to realize it would do no good.

Sheriff Dorsey picked up the gun belt and empty Colt, tossed them to his newly released prisoner, and pointed to the street door. "Go, Mr. Curry," he said, "and sin no more."

Curry didn't have to be told twice.

The following afternoon the sheriff was sitting with his feet up on his desk and thinking about whether to ask the attractive and recently widowed Sara Pennington to go with him to the barn dance next weekend when Milton Elwood stomped into the jail office, took off his battered hat, and dropped into a chair. "Sorry I'm late gettin' here, Sheriff. Wife told me you wanted to see me last night, something about a prisoner." Elwood looked at the empty cell and added, "You let him go already?"

"She," Dorsey said. "No, my deputy is delivering her to Ironwood. They'll hold her there till the judge comes through. I got no proper facilities here for women prisoners."

Elwood grunted. "Well, what'd you need from me?"

"I guess I don't need anything anymore, Milton. I was gonna ask you about that time you lived up north, and was on a posse chasing Roland Cash. Remember that?"

"Sure do. Two years ago. That was a long standoff, we had. He stayed holed up in an old mine for half a day before we got him."

Dorsey picked up a pencil and a scrap of writing paper. "So, the posse did kill him? You saw the body?"

"No, we never found a body—but the whole mine caved in on him that morning, after we shot a few holes in him." Elwood shook his head. "Devil or not, I know the man was a fierce fighter."

"Well, main thing is, he died there." Dorsey wrote R. CASH DEAD IN DAKOTA TERRITORY on the paper. "I thank you for comin' in, Milton. I should've sent word when I realized we wouldn't need to talk to you about it."

"No problem, Sheriff, I gotta stop by the hardware store anyhow." He stood and was headed for the door when Dorsey had a sudden thought.

"What do you mean, shot holes in him?"

Elwood stopped, his hand on the doorknob. "I mean we swapped a lot of lead, Cash and us, that day. Jasper Huggins shot him, I remember that, and Ezra Sims too, 'fore Cash run inside and the whole place fell in on top of him."

Sheriff Dorsey felt himself frown. "Shot him where?"

"Just outside the mine entrance."

"No, I mean where on his body?"

"Let's see . . . Huggins got him in the right leg, and Sims creased him. He was bleedin' heavy, but them scalp wounds'll do that."

Dorsey took his feet off the desk and sat up straight in his chair. "Scalp wound?"

"Yep." Elwood touched his forehead. "Just above his left eye, looked like."

Dorsey stared at the closed door a long time after Milton Elwood left. Finally, he leaned back in his chair, propped his boots again on the desktop, crumpled up the sheet of paper, and dropped it into the wastebasket.

And decided that by God he *would* ask the widow Pennington to go to the barn dance. If she turned him down, what the hell.

It wouldn't be the worst mistake he'd made lately.

At about the same time Milton Elwood was heading down the street from the sheriff's office to Farrell's Hardware, Roland Cash swung down off his horse beside a clear and gurgling stream thirty miles from the misspelled town of Longbow. He was filling his canteen and wondering which direction to take from there when he heard a rider approaching from behind, and a voice called, "Afternoon, friend." He turned to see a large man of about his own age sitting on a big buckskin with his hat tipped back from a thatch of curly hair.

Cash nodded a greeting and waited quietly for whatever would happen next. His revolver, still unloaded, was tucked out of sight along with his gun belt in his saddlebag. But the newcomer showed no sign of recognition.

"I'm Willard Lawson," the man said. "Who might you be?"

For a moment Cash considered saying Jack Curry—but recalled how well that had worked out. Taking a deep breath, he said, "Name's Roland Cash. Pleased to meet you."

"Me too," Lawson said, cheerful as could be. He paused then as if in deep thought, long enough to make Cash begin to worry a bit, and then narrowed his eyes and said, "I'm new to these parts, just here on business, but you look to me like a hard worker, Mr. Cash. You wouldn't happen to be looking, would you?"

"Looking for what?"

"Looking for work. You see, the truth is . . . well, I just bought me a cattle ranch in Australia, and—"

"Australia?"

Lawson smiled. "Yep, a ways north of a place called Melbourne. I'm putting together a crew to help me get things going down there. Got me a foreman already, plenty of stock, and some cowhands, but I need one or two more good men. You'd be gone at least a year or two, more if you like it. What do you think?"

What Cash was thinking was, *Maybe miracles do happen.* Just three days ago—not long after he'd resolved to change his ways and his life—he'd been trying to go with a different name and a different past, and he felt it might've worked had he not been weak and fallen victim to financial temptation. But he was no longer tempted in that direction and he no longer wanted to hide behind a false name and background and a different way of speaking. His newfound determination to never kill again was still as strong as ever, and who knows, if he could stay that course and earn an honest stake . . .

"Where exactly *is* Australia?" he asked.

"West," Lawson said, grinning. "A far piece west."

Cash nodded and grinned back at him. "The farther the better," he said.

*She wore clothes from a gas station, stunk of sex and bourbon,
and couldn't remember the last time she ate a vegetable.*

Meredith Craig

Don't Let the Sun Set on You (Tulsa)

When Brownie tired of dumping coins in the slot machines at the Osage Casino, she carried her beer over to a man wearing an embroidered shirt and cowboy boots. Lonely-heart hour arrived, so with limited choices, she hung around him, sipping on her drink. Blond hair combed off his face revealed features carved from mashed potatoes. When the machine's bells and whistles rang, it rained out the man's winnings, and he lifted Brownie clear off the ground and spun her around. With the promise of a bottle in one hand and an eight-ball of cocaine in the other, the man, who introduced himself as Luke, invited her back to his soon-to-be-rented hotel room.

If a man makes an offer after midnight, unless it's God, don't accept, Brownie's mother's voice warned. Her mother had been dead for years, yet she still picked fights. With rent due by Friday, Brownie waved the voice aside and Luke didn't have to ask twice before she agreed. Not terrible for a Wednesday night.

Upstairs, Luke whistled as he took in the bland hotel room with an orange bedspread, wooden furniture, and filthy carpet. "I'll tell you what, this is a nice joint," he said, plucking plastic cups from the closet-sized bathroom for the bourbon.

"I've seen worse," Brownie said. "You're a pretty lucky guy."

"Luck has nothing to do with it." Luke sat in the only chair, placing his bulging wallet and pistol on the table before dumping out powder. "It's about manifestation."

"Where'd you get that idea?" Brownie asked.

"A book called *The Power of Positive Thinking.*"

Brownie was impressed. Most guys she knew didn't read anything longer than a Reddit post.

"Ever heard of it?" he asked.

"Can't say I have." Brownie brushed her shoulder-length hair from her face and leaned on the bed's edge, more interested in the gold credit card he used to smash and methodically cut out four thin lines. He passed her a rolled ten-dollar bill he'd pulled from his wallet, and she crouched next to him, tipped her face over the line, and snorted it, relishing in the sting of her right nostril. She dipped her pinky finger in the residue and wiped it on her gums.

"So that's what you do? Read?" Brownie stood.

Luke laughed, his eyes shining. "That's not all I do. I think too." He took a line, poured the bourbon into both cups, and passed one to her.

"Oh yeah? What do you think about?"

"Lots of things. Ways to get rich, mostly."

Brownie pinched her nostrils and leaned back. The room felt in focus now, and compared to the bright lights and casino's noise, it felt quiet. She turned on the TV. They passed the time with a few more lines, and soon Brownie's jaw moved rhythmically, and she couldn't be still, her bare feet tapped the floor like Shirley Temple in dancing shoes.

The more lines Luke inhaled, the more loquacious he got. He exhilarated Brownie with his positivity and get-rich-quick schemes. He waxed about the future as though he were preaching to a congregation instead of only her. Though Brownie hadn't been to church since childhood, she found the oratory comforting.

"The trouble with most prayers is they aren't big enough. I got one idea that'll make me richer than Jeff Bezos."

Brownie scoffed. "I bet you spent your last dime on this hotel room."

"Empty pockets never held anyone back." Luke tapped his finger against his broad forehead. "Only empty minds."

"So, what's your grand idea?"

"It requires someone with a clean criminal record and a high school diploma. You know anyone like that?"

Brownie paused mid-lean, hovering the rolled bill over the table. She licked her lips.

"You graduated high school?"

"Yeah, so?" Brownie felt ridiculous for her pride. Her mother ensured she didn't make stupid mistakes like getting pregnant and dropping out of school. She'd bought her new clothes and given her a bedtime. Brownie took it for granted at the time, but now, remembering, it made her heart ache.

"You must have been sent to me from heaven."

Brownie had heard that one before, but she sat up straighter.

"Most ladies can't be trusted as far as you can throw a cat. But you're different. Your honest face makes my knees weak." He jerked up and grabbed Brownie's hands, yanking her to her feet and twirling her around the room. She couldn't help but laugh. They moved so fast, the carpet shed electricity like lightning bolts.

"If your plan's so good, how come no one's thought of it before?" she asked.

"There's always a loophole if you know where to look, and my eyes stay wide open," Luke said. "In-Home Care."

"Come again?" Brownie asked. She'd imagined a bank robbery or a kidnapping, not social services.

"Now hold on, doll," Luke said. He turned off the TV. "See here…" And in real simple terms, he explained how, after the pandemic, a shortage of elderly care workers hit the industry.

"I'm not changing diapers." Brownie frowned.

"You don't have to. And no medical training, either. Now listen…" Luke continued. "Elderly people have medicine cabinets exploding with Percocet, Morphine, Oxycontin, you name it. All free for the taking if you have a map to find it all."

"What happens to the people without their meds?" Brownie sat on the bed. She remembered her mother in the hospital with tubes up her nose and medicine to make her more comfortable.

"They re-up their prescriptions. Easy- peasy, I'll tell you what!"

Brownie thought it over, and it made sense. After a few more lines and another bourbon, she couldn't come up with one flaw in his thinking. But she wasn't the right person for the job. She took a mental inventory of her dyed black hair, fake lashes, neon leggings, and the cold sore growing above her top lip. "Who's going to hire me?"

"Without confidence, you can't succeed."

In Luke's coal-black eyes, Brownie saw a sureness she wanted to possess. Ever since her mother had passed, she'd been waiting for someone like him to come along and take care of her, someone to invite her back to the promised land, a version of America that included security, direction, and someone to hold her hand and pretend everything would be all right.

The seatbelts in Luke's truck were broken and he drove fast. As he sped around the curves, Brownie clutched the door handle while the dashboard bobblehead of Dale Earnhardt Jr. swung on its spring. The Oklahoma landscape whipped past them, hurtling towards the Kansas border. Brownie wanted to wait a day before launching the plan, but she needed rent money. Anyway, Luke said, "When gold diggers struck big, did they wait for a good night's sleep before lining their pockets? Hell, no!" There was a difference between panning for gold and a job interview, but Luke insisted they were the same. "If you don't jump on this opportunity, someone else will. And you'll be left with nothing but regret."

Brownie knew a thing or two about that, as bad decisions peppered her life. If she could do it over, she'd make different decisions, like settling for less when motivated guys like Luke were available. His life charged through endless green arrows while hers blinked at a broken stop light, never gaining forward momentum.

She'd showered, changed into clothes Luke purchased from the gas station, a clean T-shirt emblazoned with the casino brand and a pair of khaki shorts. She resembled a casino employee. Luke said she'd hit the nail on the head. "It's easier to get a job if you already have one."

From the plastic sack in the center console's cup holder, Brownie took a quick bump of powder with her fingernail. Her stomach twitched with nerves, hollow from a diet of brown liquor, beer, and cocaine. Luke offered her an ibuprofen he'd bought at the gas station to even it out, but instead, she wrestled a loose Xanax from her purse and swallowed it dry.

Luke snorted a bump while driving and described the personality she'd need to present at the interview. "You think on your feet, and won't let anything stand in your way!"

Like a coach in a boxing ring, he gave her a pep talk. By the time they swung into the parking lot in front of a squat building set back from the busy road, Brownie almost felt eligible for the job. All she needed was a high school diploma, a clean record, and a valid driver's license, all of which she had. She wasn't lying or cheating. About that, anyways. The only untruth was fibbing about the year's experience at a nursing home. Luke's California cell phone number would be the reference.

"Easy-peasy," Luke said.

Brownie popped down the mirror and applied another coat of lipstick over her cold sore. Her mother's voice echoed in the car, *It's like putting lipstick on a pig.* She wiped a smudge of stray eyeliner. What kind of people applied for this job?

"I'll tell you what, they'll be glad to see you." Luke kissed Brownie, his tongue dry and his skin damp.

At a quarter past ten, Brownie opened the truck door to the hot air; the breeze only kicked up dust. Her heels clicked on the pavement, her body heavy from sleep deprivation. The building, a bunker with tiny windows, didn't possess curb appeal. She didn't want to go in. Behind her, the glass' glare obscured Luke, but she imagined him egging her on with words of wisdom. *Listen to your gut.* Her mother said this in both figurative and literal ways. She distrusted Brownie's father before uncovering his affair and subsequent abandonment, and then, years later, she visited a doctor with stomach pain complaints and a year later, that's what killed her.

Under the "Home Care Center" sign Brownie opened the

door to a blast of cold air which sucked her into an office where an obese woman in a checkered tank perched behind a desk, pecking on the computer, the batwings of her arms flapping. The fluorescent lights illuminated Brownie's hangover, exposing the filth under her clean clothes.

"Can I help you?" The woman stared down her nose at Brownie.

"I'm looking for work," Brownie said before remembering Luke insisted she be upbeat. She wished she'd taken another bump. "I'm an in-home care worker."

"You fill out an application online. You don't come here."

Brownie tapped her foot. Luke would be angry if she returned with her tail between her legs. "Well, see, I didn't realize, and I'm here now. I've got experience and references and all that." Her skin crawled and she willed herself not to scratch, not to move her jaw or make any sudden movements while the woman evaluated her for red flags.

"What kind of experience?" The woman paused. "Take a seat. I've got time for an intake." The woman heaved herself off the chair and moved down the hall. The computer screensaver, a cat in a snowsuit, blinked on before she returned.

Brownie didn't expect the woman to have her fill out an application, fax over her high school diploma, clear her background check and call her reference right in front of her, but as she sat across the desk stinking of booze, she heard Luke's tinny voice on the receiver's other end.

"I'll tell you what, she was the best worker we had. One of our residents spread feces all over the dang place, and she marched in there and told him what's what. Plus, she's on time. Good work ethic."

"Thank you, Mr—"

"Now, you call me back if you have any other questions."

The woman hung up the phone and pinched her chin. "Most of our patients require assistance with their IADLs by their PCA, so we could start you off with Respite Care. It's only a couple hours a day, but can potentially turn into overnights."

Brownie's eyes glazed over. The scam's excitement wore off, and she resented being in this claustrophobic office space. The woman stapled copies of Brownie's vaccine card, faxed high school diploma, and application.

"You need some water, hon?" the woman asked, taking in Brownie's jaw, working itself into a grind.

When the woman stood to get a Dixie cup, Brownie gave in to scratching and tore up her upper arms under the sleeves of her T-shirt.

"Now, we're short staffed and I assume you got experience with sundowning, so you should be fine with difficult patients." The woman passed Brownie the water.

Desperate to leave the freezing room, Brownie stood.

"I'll print the address and your list of duties." The woman turned to busy herself with administrative actions, and Brownie drank the thimble of water and sucked in her teeth. "Call if you have any problems."

The woman handed her the assignment, and Brownie practically exploded out the door, stopping herself from running across the parking lot in case the woman was spying out the window. When she neared the truck, she couldn't help sprinting to Luke's door, jumping into his lap where he welcomed her like she'd cured cancer instead of scamming an entry-level job. They fucked in the truck's front seat, and Brownie half-wished the woman would appear at the window, her fat face rearranged in shock and disgust. Brownie came noisily with the threat of being caught invoking the adolescent thrill of basement sex at a parents' house.

When they finished, Luke eased the car onto the highway and drove to the shady side of a Walmart parking lot where they could doze for a few hours until the shift. Brownie wanted to do a few more lines, but there wasn't anymore, and besides, Luke insisted they rest. She took another Xanax instead. He rolled down the windows an inch, lay back their seats, and pulled a brimmed hat from the backseat over his pockmarked face. In no time at all, Luke snored, and Brownie twitched in her seat, slipping in and out of consciousness until the afternoon sun baked the car like a casserole and the time for the shift arrived.

Brownie didn't know what she expected, but it wasn't the well-maintained ranch they pulled up in front of. A dogwood tree commanded respect from the yard's left corner though most of its blooms had fallen. In a different part of Oklahoma, she'd grown up in a similar-style house. She remembered what it felt like to live on solid ground, in a place you could return to, year after year and observe the vegetation change. In that way, it could have been a homecoming, but instead, it only highlighted how far she'd fallen from being the kind of person who'd live in a house like this. She wore clothes from a gas station, stunk of sex and bourbon, and couldn't remember the last time she ate a vegetable. If only her mother could see her now.

"I can't go in there," she said to herself, as much as to Luke.

"Say howdy and excuse yourself to the bathroom. Swap the pills with these." He passed her the supersized bottle of ibuprofen he'd scored at the gas station. "When you're done, we'll celebrate at a steakhouse."

"I'm not wearing this to a fancy restaurant." Brownie made a face at her wrinkled khakis.

"Alrighty. We'll order room service instead. You won't need

a lick of clothing." He leaned in to kiss her neck. "Don't get any ideas about cutting me out, now. When you switch the pills, come back out here." Brownie exited the vehicle and leaned her head back in to kiss him, happy for the smear of lipstick she left behind. As she walked up the drive, Luke hollered after her, "Manifest, baby doll!"

She rang the doorbell, and when no one answered, she pushed open the unlocked door. "Hello?" she called out.

Inside, the dim and cool house overpowered Brownie with the smell of roses. Heavily polished furniture crowded the entryway and sunken living room. She passed through the foyer's sitting area, and her eyes snagged on a candy bowl filled with butterscotch. The house was dead silent. She picked up framed photos of family members and imagined the old woman's child had swung by to treat her to dinner. Brownie crept around the room and backed up the stairs to the kitchen, spotless with beige appliances humming quietly. Off the kitchen, a pantry held neatly stacked cans of soup next to toilet paper, paper towels, and garbage can liners. She pilfered a plastic bag and continued to the half bath. *A powder room,* her mother's voice corrected her. Inside, no medicine cabinet, only an oval mirror in a decorative frame.

Back through the foyer, she traversed the other direction, down a hallway, past three doors, behind which she assumed were bedrooms. Ahead of her, another bathroom, with the door flung open. The plush carpet muffled her footsteps. Mauve tile decorated dual sinks in a thirty-year-old bathroom while medical equipment and bottles of pills littered the countertops. Brownie's heart beat faster. One medicine cabinet yawned open. Diazepam. Morphine. Lorazepam. Brownie tugged out the bottles and swallowed a few yellow pills, figuring they'd help her finish the job. She counted out pills, replaced them with ibuprofen, and dumped the medication in the plastic liner bag from the pantry as methodically as a grocery bagger. How smoothly Luke's plan had gone, how easy to earn rent money. *Stepped in shit and came out smelling like a rose,* her mother's voice whispered. The painstaking and time-consuming work bored her, but she continued until only a few bottles remained. When her fingers felt thick and clumsy, the pills she'd swallowed kicked in. Her eyes fluttered, and she fought back an urge to lean over the toilet and vomit. She didn't want to make any noise or mess up the spotless house. Sweat beaded across her chest.

"You've come home?' a female voice rang out. Not her mother's this time. A woman in a floral house dress and robe appeared, eyes bulging, and a shock of white hair stuck out from her visible scalp. "Give me a hug, why don't you?" the woman asked, her voice frail, her arms spread. She blocked Brownie's exit to the front door.

Brownie's stomach muscles tensed, forcing stomach acid up, and she leaned heavily against the counter to dry heave into the sink. Unsure what to say, Brownie held fast to the bag of pills and pulled herself through the door. "I'm your aide," Brownie said with garbled language, mysterious sounds on her furry tongue. She shuffled forward outside the bathroom, attempting to pass the woman and get outside.

The woman pivoted, gnarled bare feet curled into the rug, and she clutched Brownie in an awkward embrace. "I'm happy you're here. So happy."

The woman's pigeon bones poked through her thin robe, and her arms were like talons fastening Brownie to her papery onion skin. Brownie's stomach clenched and unclenched, remembering her mother's engulfing embrace. After a moment, Brownie attempted to pull away, but her wooziness couldn't compete with the old woman's strength. They stood in the hallway for minutes, swaying a bit.

Brownie's shoulders relaxed, and a shudder passed through her body. And another. Her body drooped over the woman. Vomit dribbled from her mouth, unnoticed, onto the bathrobe. The stench of her insides mingled with the woman's rose scent and the faint musk of her mother's perfume. *You're my best girl.*

Movement from down the hall made Brownie flinch, and she pried open her eyes, a metallic taste stung her mouth. Luke's silhouette appeared in the foyer, a shadow moving towards them. "What the hell?"

Dampness streaked Brownie's face, and her mouth prickled with dryness. Her lips opened and closed, her heart slowed, and her lungs strained for breath. The old woman made a sound like "ou ou ou" and let go of Brownie to face Luke.

"I'll tell you what, I don't have a good feeling about this. You two acquainted?" Luke's pistol drew a line between Brownie and the woman.

"Leave my daughter alone!" The woman spoke in a loud voice.

"What?" Luke's features rearranged into unfamiliar lumps as he paced the foyer. His jaw tightened; his black eyes bloodshot. Brownie shook her head, her own eyes heavy.

"I know what you want, and you're not getting it." The woman stood in front of Brownie with her arms spread as if she could protect Brownie from a firing squad. The blue veins under her white skin bulged, and pink bile dribbled from her hair and shoulder.

"There's no such thing as defeat."

"I called the police! They're coming!"

One of Luke's hands balled in a fist and the other hammered the gun's butt against the wallpaper. "What. The. Actual. Fuck. Is. Going. On?" Each word emphasized with a strike.

Brownie stumbled against the wall, her mouth moving like a guppy in need of water. If she could speak, she'd comfort Luke or ask him to call an ambulance because her muscles resembled sandbags.

The woman shrieked. "Don't you touch us!"

As if hearing an invitation in her words, Luke headed towards them, the gun scuffing the wall where it dragged, drawing nearer.

"Get out of here! The police are on their way!" The woman transformed into action, jumping, landing on Luke, her nails at his face. "Ou ou ou ou." The two spun around as if dancing. Too late for positive thinking. Luke grunted and heaved forward to propel the woman off and slam her down to the floor. An explosion, like the woman's head cracked open, deafened Brownie for a minute. Then the woman continued to scream. Brownie felt a tightness in her chest, like a game she played in the pool with her mother, to hold their breaths underwater to see who'd stay submerged the longest. She crashed to the floor with the bag of pills catching her fall.

In the bathroom, Luke rifled through the cabinets, grabbing the containers meticulously replaced by Brownie. If only she'd explained the pills, if only the woman stopped making those sounds, he wouldn't be so mad. Luke moved too fast to catch. She held her breath, her hand twitched.

"I'll tell you what, I've never seen anyone so full of negativity." He stepped over the two women as easily as avoiding dog shit in brand-new boots. In the foyer, the front door slammed shut, the vibrations toppled the candy dish. Brownie pined for the butterscotch, imagining the taste of caramelized sugar darkening her tongue, melting in her mouth like a church wafer from the priest's hand. *Say Amen,* her mother's voice scolded her. In the driveway, the truck's engine turned over and groaned away.

The elderly woman settled down as the daylight faded from the hallway. She busied herself with blotting the sticky crimson stains around Brownie's body with her robe. Minutes passed. She cradled Brownie in her arms and stroked her face until Brownie's vision pinholed. *Time to go home now. Time to go.*

Authors

In Order of Appearance

Alec Cizak is a writer and filmmaker from Indianapolis. His fiction has appeared in several journals and anthologies. He is also the editor of the fiction journal Pulp Modern.

Michael Bracken is the Edgar Award- and Shamus Award-nominated, Derringer-winning author of 1,200 short stories, including crime fiction published in *Alfred Hitchcock's Mystery Magazine*, *Ellery Queen's Mystery Magazine*, *The Best American Mystery Stories*, and *The Best Mystery Stories of the Year*. Additionally, he is the Anthony Award-nominated editor of more than twenty published and forthcoming anthologies, the editor of *Black Cat Mystery Magazine*, and is an associate editor of *Black Cat Weekly*. He lives, writes, and edits in Texas.

Tom Hoisington is a journalist living in West Salem, OR, with his wife, daughter, and cats.

Christine Boyer has been published in *The Little Patuxent Review*, *The Tahoma Literary Review*, and *So It Goes: the Literary Journal of the Kurt Vonnegut Museum and Library*, among others. Her essay "Second Person" was named a notable essay of 2020 in the *Best American Essays* anthology. She lives in Massachusetts, and she can be found at christine-boyer.com.

Russell Thayer's work has appeared in *Brushfire*, *The Phoenix*, *Evening Street Review*, *Cirque*, *Close to the Bone*, *Bristol Noir*, *Apocalypse Confidential*, *Hawaii Pacific Review*, *Shotgun Honey*, *Punk Noir*, *Pulp Modern*, and *Tough*. He received his BA in English from the University of Washington, worked for decades at large printing companies, and currently lives in Missoula, Montana.

Matt Phillips lives in San Diego. His crime novels include *Know Me from Smoke*, *Countdown*, *You Must Have a Death Wish*, and *Three Kinds of Fool*.

Trevor Holliday's series of six crime novels featuring supercool private investigator Frank Trinity are set in 1980s Tucson. His stand-alone novels *Lefty and the Killers* and *Ferguson's Trip* take readers to northern Maine and *Dim Lights Thick Smoke* explores Holbrook, Arizona along Route 66. *Ten Shots Quick*, a collection of linked neo-western stories, will be published this summer. Holliday has lived most of his life in northern Arizona. He and his wife now live in Erie, Pennsylvania.

As a filmmaker, writer, and artist, **Ian Klink**'s work include the feature film *Anybody's Blues*, his thesis film adaptation of Stephen King's *The Man Who Would Not Shake Hands*, and short stories for *The Creeps* magazine and *Chilling Tales For Dark Nights*. Klink shares his talents as a teacher of Computer technology/Multimedia studies in Pennsylvania.

January Bain has been fascinated with words since childhood when her mother took the time to read a chapter a night to her children from wonderful adventure books. She writes poetry, songs, and novels in a number of genres, has won an award for her mystery/thriller work, been blessed by her novels having been translated into other languages, with some in the process of being made into games. She first and foremost considers herself a storyteller, obsessed with understanding the motivations of her characters to bring her stories and poems to life. She hopes to inspire and touch hearts.

Burke De Boer is an Oregon-grown, Texas-based writer and horticulturist. His short fiction has appeared in *Cowboy Jamboree*, *Roi Fainéant*, and *BULL Magazine*. You can find his western novel, *In Sheep's Clothing*, and his music review, *Interstellar Wannabes: A Glitch Rock Retrospective*, at thirdeyesockeye.com. You can also find him on Twitter @burkedeboer

Joseph S. Walker lives in Indiana and teaches college literature and composition courses. His short fiction has appeared in *Alfred Hitchcock's Mystery Magazine*, *Ellery Queen's Mystery Magazine*, *Mystery Weekly*, *Tough*, and a number of other magazines and anthologies, including three consecutive editions of *The Mysterious Bookshop Presents the Best Mystery Stories of the Year*. He has been nominated for the Edgar Award and the Derringer Award and has won the Bill Crider Prize for Short Fiction. He also won the Al Blanchard Award in 2019 and 2021. Follow him on Twitter @JSWalkerAuthor and visit his website at jswalkerauthor.com.

John M. Floyd's work has appeared in more than 350 different publications, including *Alfred Hitchcock's Mystery Magazine*, *Ellery Queen's Mystery Magazine*, *Strand Magazine*, *The Saturday Evening Post*, and four editions of Otto Penzler's best-mysteries-of-the-year anthologies. A former Air Force captain and IBM systems engineer, John is an Edgar finalist, a Shamus Award winner, a five-time Derringer Award winner, a three-time Pushcart Prize nominee, and the author of nine books. He is also the 2018 recipient of the Short Mystery Fiction Society's lifetime achievement award.

Meredith Craig, a Brooklyn writer, has work published in *Fictive Dream*, *Stanchion Journal*, *Variety Pack*, *Rock Salt Journal*, *Scribble Lit*, and anthologized in *Jacked: A Crime Anthology* published by Run Amok Books. Her work has been nominated for "Best of the Net 2023" and "The 2023 Best American Mystery and Suspense" series. Additionally, her non-fiction travel pieces have appeared in *Lonely Planet, Delta Sky, Vice,* among others, and she has written and produced for television. She tweets at @meredithcraigde and can be found at meredithcraigdepietro.com.